Sarah Robinson Reid

Immortelles

Sarah Robinson Reid

Immortelles

ISBN/EAN: 9783337374983

Printed in Europe, USA, Canada, Australia, Japan

Cover: Foto ©Andreas Hilbeck / pixelio.de

More available books at **www.hansebooks.com**

Immortelles

A Tribute to the "Old South."

A compilation by

Sarah Robinson R

PREFACE.

Before offering these pages for publication, I have endeavored to learn if there is in print another book covering the same ground. The field is wide, and many of the songs and memorials in this collection are here recorded for the first time. It has been my object, as near as possible, to arrange the matter in consecutive order, beginning with the seceding of the Southern States and concluding with the close of the war. To every section of our broad Southland all honor shall be given—her chieftain, gallant officers and private soldiers—their deeds shall speak for them.

The traditions and wars of Greece were glorified by poetry and song—invested with new life by the immortal Homer; their authors became historians.

Historians may record the great events of a nation's history with accuracy, but in describing motive and defining sentiment they are not unfrequently influenced by prejudices peculiar to their own environment and education. Hence, in the spontaneous poetry and song of a nation we find at last the true exponent to motive and action. Moral accountability must always be determined by honesty of intention and purity of motive, however far from the right may be our conclusion; and, while the passionate political debates during the war, and pages of history written since the close, may be colored by other influences, it is certain that the poetry and song that burst spontaneous from the Southern heart manifested the true spirit and motive. No nation had more inspiring war songs than did the Confederate States of America. "Tell it as you may, it never can be told." These songs are treasured by the old veterans as sacred. Upon Southern field and hillside, where heroes fell, while chanting their refrain, their echoes died away as the sun of the Confederacy—like the setting of a great hope, went down; yet the stars came out and shone above their graves, and in the silence we catch again the echo, and in song their spirits live, while once more—

> The sweet bird of the South
> Might build in every cannon's mouth,
> Till the only sound from its rusty throat
> Should be the wren's and bluebird's note.

Now that a united nation stands under one

glorious flag, the deeds of her heroes North and South must be our common hertitage.

> Discord with the battle ends.
> In peace, they wonder why the battle rose,
> And ask how souls so great could e'r be foes;
> The hardy veteran, proud of many a scar,
> The manly charms and honors of the war,
> Leans on his spear to take a farewell view;
> And, sighing, bids the glorious camp adieu.

S. R.

Immortelles.

By Sarah Robinson Reid.

NATIONAL SONG—THE MAGNOLIA.

Albert Pike.

What, what is the true Southern symbol—
  The symbol of Honor and Right;
The emblem that suits a brave people
  In arms against numbers and might?
'Tis the ever green stately Magnolia,
  Its pearl flowers pure as the truth;
Defiant of tempest and lightning.
  It's life a perpetual youth.

Chorus—Our colors, the blue, white and green.
        Independence and freedom forever.
        Hurrah! for the blue, white and green.

French blood stained with glory the lillies,
  While centuries marched to their grave,
And over-bold Scot and gay Irish
  The thistle and shamrock yet wave;
Ours, ours, be the noble Magnolia,
  That only on Southern soil grows.
The symbol of life everlasting.
  Leave the Eagle to strive for our foes.

Chorus—Our colors, the blue, white and green.
        Independence and freedom forever.
        Hurrah! for the blue, white and green!

A Flag Presentation.

At Belmonte, Ala., the following young ladies stepped forward, representing the seceding States, as they left the Old Confederacy, carrying with them the rights and privileges bequeathed them by their ancestors of the Revolution. One by one they repeated the following appropriate and patriotic lines:

SOUTH CAROLINA—REPRESENTED BY MISS MATILDA FENNEL.

> First to rise against oppression
>   In the glorious Southern band.
> Home of dead and living heroes,
>   South Carolina takes her stand.

MISSISSIPPI—MISS CORNIE COPERTON.

> Sisters, room for Mississippi;
>   Well she knows the martial chain.
> She has marched of old to battle,
>   She will strike her foes again.

TEXAS—MISS PARTHENIA BRYANT.

> Texas, youngest 'mid her sisters,
>   Joins her earnest voice to theirs.
> Forth she sends her gallant rangers
>   With her blessings and her prayers.

VIRGINIA—MISS SALLIE FENNEL.

> Wave, wave on high your banners,
>   For the Old Dominion comes,
> With her lightning speaking thunder;
>   Lo! where sound her army's drums.

NORTH CAROLINA—MISS JENNIE ARMSTRONG.

Over vail and over mountain,
    Pealing forth the trumpest high,
Comes a lofty swell of music,
    The old North State's battle cry.

ARKANSAS—MISS SALLIE CARTER.

Long Arkansas waited, hoping,
    Clinging to the flag of stars,
Now she tears them down forever;
    Ho! away then for the wars.

TENNESSEE—MISS KATE MATTOX.

Last, but far from least, among ye
    Spartan band of brave and free,
Like a whirlwind in her anger,
    Wheels in line old Tennessee.

FIRST CONFEDERATE SHOT.

THE very first life lost in the final direct struggle over secession, was on the Federal side at Fort Sumpter, in an accidental explosion after the fort had surrendered April 13, 1861. But the first Confederate to be killed in battle was Private Henry Lawson Wyatt. a soldier in Company A, First North Carolina Infantry. His life was lost in the battle known as "Big Bethel." fought June 10, 1861, near Yorktown, Va. The conflict at "Big Bethel" was the first land battle of the war. Though on a minor scale it was a brilliant victory for the Southern arms. The Confederate troops engaged belonged to the command of General John B. Magruder, the infantry force being chiefly the North Carolina regiment under the immediate command of Colonel D. H. Hill, who was afterwards a Lieutenant-General in the Confederate service, and was regarded as the hero of the battle. The Lieutenant-Colonel of the regiment was C. C. Lee and the Major was James H. Lane, both of whom subsequently rose to the rank of Brigadier General in the Confederacy. The regiment passed into history as the Bethel Regiment of North Carolina troops.

Battery of Richmond Howitzers was in command of Captain W. W. Randolph, who subsequently became the Confederate Secretary of War, and whose face afterward appeared on the paper currency. The Federal forces, several thousand troops engaged in action, was under the immediate command of General B. F. Butler.

Henry Wyatt was a native of Virginia, born in Richmond February 12. 1842. He was one of the very first men to enlist as a soldier for the Southern cause when the Governor of North Carolina called for volunteers in April, 1861, after the Lincoln proclamation declaring war against the Southern States. He entered the Edgecomb Guards under command of Captain John L. Bridges. Fifty-four days after he was mustered into service, Henry Wyatt fell in battle at the age of 20. He was burried near the foot of the Cornwallis monument, Yorktown, Va. Virginia should see that a fitting memorial is erected over the grave of her heroic son. In the beginning of the battle the sharp-shooters of the enemy occupied a house between the two opposing lines—blue and gray.

A call was made for volunteers to advance across the intervening distance through an open field, two hundred yards wide, and fire the building. Privates Wyatt, John H. Thorpe, George Williams and a youth named Taylor responded to the call. They had proceeded but a short distance when Henry Wyatt fell with a bullet in his brain from a volley fired from the building.

The other three soldiers dropped to the ground and remained until Captain Randolph, bringing his guns to bear upon the building, destroyed it and opened a way for the Confederate forward movement.

The comrades of young Wyatt rejoined their command, went through the war and are yet living. Very soon after the cannonading of the house began Major Winthrop, a gallant and noble son of Connecticut, endeavored to lead his men into action, but as he came to the front, waving his sword about his head, the North Carolinians fired a volley and he fell dead—he, I believe, the first victim among the Federal officers of the war. His native State has long ago perpetuated his memory.

Enlisted To-Day.

(Found on the body of a young soldier, Alabama regiment.)

I know the sun shines and the lilacs are blowing,
  And summer sends kisses to beautiful May.
On, to see all the treasures the spring is bestowing,
  And to think my boy, Willie, enlisted to-day.

It seems but a day since, the twilight low humming,
  I rocked him to sleep with his cheek upon mine,
While Robbie, the four-year-old, watched for the coming
Of father adown the street's indistinct line.

It is many a year since my Harry departed
  To come back no more in the twilight or dawn
And Robbie grew weary of watching and started
  Alone in the journey his father had gone.

It is many a year, and this afternoon sitting
  At Robbie's old window I heard the band play,
And suddenly ceased dreaming over my knitting
  To reccollect Willie is twenty to-day.

And that standing beside him this soft May day morning,
  The sun making gold of his wreathed cigar smoke,
I saw in the sweet eyes and lips a faint warning
  And choked down the tears when he eagerly spoke.

"Dear mother, you know how the north-men are crowing.
  They would trample the rights of the South in the dust.
The boys are all fire; they wish I were going."
  He stopped, but his eyes said: "Oh, say if I must?"

I smiled on the boy, though my heart it seemed breaking·
  My eyes filled with tears as I turned them away
And answered: "Willie, 'tis well you are waking.
  Go act as your father would bid you to-day."

I sit at the window and see the flags flying
  And dreamily list to the roll of the drum,
And smother the pain in my heart that is lying
  And bid.all the fears in my bosom be dumb.

I shall sit at the window when summer is lying
  Out over the fields and the honey bees' hum
Lulls the rose at the porch from her tremulous sighing
  And watch for the face of my darling to come.

And if he should fall his young life he has given
  For freedom's sweet sake, and for me I will pray
Once more with my Harry and Robbie in heaven
  To meet the dear boy that enlisted to-day.

The Origin of Dixie.

Some years ago, before the war, a very musical family by the name of Dixie lived in Worcester, Mass. One of the brothers, Walston Dixie, we believe, decided to apply his talents in the negro minstrelsy line. and soon the famous "Dixie Minstrels" were known from one end of

the country to the other.　This same founder of
the troupe wrote the 'celebrated song "Dixie's
Land," which attained such popularity.　He
found in the Southern States the germs of the
quaint negro songs, which he brushed up and
placed in his programme.　The South adopted
the song, and hence allowed this gifted minstrel
of Massachusetts to give that section of the
country a new name, which will always stick.
Many songs have been adopted and sectionized
in this way.　"Yankee Doodle" was written by
an Englishman as a satire. but our ancestors
picked it up and gave it a home.

Another Version—Author of Dixie.

Daniel Decatur Emmett, the author of Dixie.
was born at Mt. Vernon, Knox County, Ohio,
on the 29th of October. 1815.　The word
"Dixie" is said to have been started from a
Mr. Dix, a typical Southerner.　He inaugurated.
however. the blacking of faces. which had much
to do with the popularity of his Dixie "Walk
'Round."

Dixie's Land—"Walk 'Round."

Composed by Daniel D. Emmett for Bryant's Minstrels.

> I wish I was in the land ob cotton,
> Cinnamon seed and sandy bottom,
> 　Look away, look away, away Dixie land.
> Dixie land where I was born in,
> Early on one frosty mornin',

Look away, away, look away, Dixie land.
Den I wish I was in Dixie, hooray, hooray,
  Dixie's land we'll take our stand,
To lib and die in Dixie, away, away,
  Away down South in Dixie.

Old missus marry Will, the weaber.
William was a gay deceaber—
When he put his arms around her,
He look as fierce as a forty pounder.
  Chorus—Hooray, hooray, etc.

His face was sharp as a butcher's cleaber,
But dat did not seem to greab her;
Will run away, missus took a decline, O,
Her face was the color of bacon rhine, O.
  Chorus—Hooray, hooray, etc.

While missus libbed she libbed in clover,
When she died she died all ober;
How could she act such a foolish part, O,
And marry a man to break her heart, O.
  Chorus--Hooray, hooray, etc.

Bucketwheat cake and stony batter
Makes you fat or a little fatter;
Here's a health to the new ole missus,
An' all de gals dat wants to kiss us.
  Chorus—Hooray, hooray, etc.

Now, if you want to drive 'way sorrow,
Come and hear dis song to-morrow,
Den hoe it down and scratch your grabble.
To Dixie's land I'm bound to trabble.
  Chorus—Hooray, hooray, etc.

Mr. Emmett was known in his minstrel character as "Uncle Dan." He said Jerie Bryant told him to make a song the boys can whoop and holler—a regular negro walk round. "The

next day (Sunday) I sat down with my violin
while it rained and composed 'Dixe Land.' "

OUR DIXIE.

BY A LADY OF AUGUSTA, GA., 1865.

I heard long since a simple strain.
It brought no thrill of joy or pain;
Nor did I care to hear again
    Of Dixie.

But time rolled on, and drum and fife
Gave token of a coming strife,
And called our youth to soldier life
    In Dixie.

And so our treasures, one by one,
All by the battlefield were won.
They heard at morn and setting sun—
    Our Dixie.

Their blood flowed on the fresh green hill,
It mingled with the mountain rill
And poured through vales once calm and still
    In Dixie.

The living rallied to their stand,
Their war cry was their "Native Land,"
But sadder from their lessening land
    Came Dixie.

Yet still it roused to deeds of fame
And made immortal many a name,
It never caused a blush of shame—
    Our Dixie.

We may not hear that simple strain
Ever without a thrill of pain—
Our dead come back to live again
    With Dixie.

And if I were a generous foe
I'd honor him whose heart's best throe,
Leaped to that music soft and low—
    Our Dixie.

First Confederate Flag.

Mr. Christopher Nelson claimed that the first Confederate flag had been raised by him. and referred to Mr. Lee Howard. who said: "On the afternoon of the 5th of March. 1861, Mr. Colcock, then collector of the port. received from Wm. Porcher Miles. Montgomery. Ala., then the capital of the Confederacy, a telegram giving the design just determined on by that body for the Confederate flag. I suggested to him to have one made at once and have it hoisted the next morning over the custom house. To this Mr. Colcock demurred, whereupon I ordered the porter, Christopher Nelson, to make one for me that night. To my surprise and pleasure I saw it next day, March 6, 1861, flying on the staff of the custom house. Captain Tom Lockwood requested the loan of it for his steamer for Florida, the first to float over her waters.

A Flag Presentation.

BY SALLIE ROBINSON.

Gentlemen—For and in behalf of the ladies of this city, I present you this flag. It has been adopted as the ensign of the Confederate States. Its existence is attributable alone to the existence of that spirit of freedom in the Southern heart which animated and cheered our fathers in the struggle for independence. Believing this, we have the utmost confidence that your strength will be devoted to its defense when attacked by the millions of a party who have for years been studiously working the ruin of the fair fabric of American independence — the Union, which work is now complete. The Union is at an end. Although we are not so intimately identified with the nation over which it floats as is desirable, yet we look forward to the time when we shall be a component part of it, and claim the equal privileges of its constitution and laws, thus relieving ourselves of the thought of being subjugated.

The dread horrors of war are far preferable to subjugation and degradation. To the dastard the prospect of war brings a shudder, but to us servility and negro equality is far more alarming.

That the rights of the South have been invaded there can be no question, and the only excuse for him who now shrieks for the Union is *fear*. In this crisis, we pledge you, fear has no abiding place in our heart. We speak not alone for ourselves, but for the ladies of Johnson County. Although they have been reared in the once happy Union and enjoyed all the blessings of peace and prosperity to which our nation had attained, yet we have the same stern inflexibility in our natures which, in our mothers, gave so much of confidence to the soldier and citizen in the darkest hour of the Revolution.

Although not accustomed to hardships, we have the fortitude to endure them if likely to be productive of good. You who are strong battle for the right, and you shall have such assistance as within us lies. Without designing compliment to ourselves, history shows that whenever or wherever the flag of liberty has been unfurled our sex have been its strongest admirers and supporters.

Unfurl this flag as we present it to you. Within its folds are designs directive of the thoughts to the struggle now being made for freedom in the South. Hoist it, and long may it wave. May the nation of which it is an ensign be fostered and our own independence be established under its protective policy. May our fondest and brightest hopes of the future prosperity and protective glory of the nation over which it floats be fully consummated in the full enjoyment by the people of the blessings of liberty once purchased by the blood of our fathers. May this flag never trail in the dust.

[We are sorry not to be able to give the very appropriate response to the flag presentation by Dr. J. P. Mitchell on that day of sunshine never fairer in Arkansas. The music of Dixie rever-

berated through the hills and valleys of Spadra's
stream.   The air was redolent with the fragrance
of orchard blossoms and spring-time flowers; not
a glimpse of the shadow of war's desolation darkened the landscape.   Every heart beat high with
hope and courage.   Though not her own com-
position, they were, seemingly, bold, brave
words to fall from the lips of the little school-
girl "miss" who stood upon the platform in the
courtyard.   What knew she of the horrors of
civil war?   As much as many of that brave band
of Clarksville boys, looking so handsome in their
"minute" men caps, ready to do battle for their
country, by whom she was surrounded.   It mattered not, the address was inspiring; and as the
speaker flung out words of defiance to those who
dare invade our homes, a humming bird—fairy
bird of the Southland—fluttered nearer and
nearer, captivated by their sweetness, and rested
on the flowers at her throat—a bright, happy
omen.   In the years to come that scene may
be blotted from the memory by war's tempest
of tears, fire and blood, the South made desolate,
her homes in ashes, but her sons will not tamely
submit; they know no servile fear.   Forever
sacred the soil where her heroes fall, immortal
their fame!—S. R., Clarksville.]

For Miss Sallie Robinson.

The battle strife is resounding
  Through the American land;
The fiery cannon is rebounding;
  The conflicts brilliant and grand.

There is magic in the cry, "To arms!"
  To do battle for our soil;
To face the enemy's alarms,
  To wade through many a toil.

The soldier suffers much and long,
  And has his heart wrung often.
Although his arm is good and strong,
  His feeling heart will soften

When he thinks of those dear ones
  He fondly desires to see.
Let us pray for the patriot sons
  Who fight and strive the South to free.

Let us pray the "God of Battles"
  Our patriot friends to shield,
And, while the iron hail rattles,
  Brace their arms their swords to wield.

May the foe be driven to flight
  And the weary conflict cease,
Our land be ever blest with right,
  Freedom, contentment and peace.

J. S. Powers.

Clarksville, Ark., Oct. 20, 1861.

Dear Sallie—In writing my name in your book of remembrance, I will record the placing the "Star of Arkansas" the tenth in number in the glorious constellation of the "Confederated States of America." As the flag of your city ascended in the air this afternoon for more than

a hundred feet, the balmy south wind filling its
ample folds, for the first time we saw with joy
in the bright galaxy the star of Arkansas. May
this beautiful flag, through all the years to come,
wave in peace and proud tranquility over your
home and mine.

MAGGIE CUNNINGHAM.

Clarksville, Ark., May 9, 1861.

THE CONFEDERATE GRAY UNIFORM.

GENERAL RUFUS SAXTON.

IT is not generally known that the Confederate
uniform was designed at West Point. It hap-
pened in this way: I was an instructor of
artillery at the Academy from May 1, 1859, to
September, 1860. General S. B. Buckner, who
was Adjutant-General of Kentucky, came here for
the purpose of obtaining a new uniform for the
troops of that State. We agreed that the hand-
somest uniform was the Cadet gray. Buckner
went South and the uniform we had decided
upon became that of the Confederate army. W.
H. Bemess writes from Shelbyville, Ky.: "I do
not know whether General Saxton is right about
it, but I am inclined to think he is. I do know,

however, that Kentucky had State troops (State Guards) at that time (1859–60) under General Buckner, and they (at least some of them) were uniformed in cadet gray. The uniform was not furnished by the State. Each man paid for his own uniform. I was a member of a company of State Guards (Stone Rifles), at Bloomfield, Nelson County, Kentucky. Most of us went South wearing our cadet gray uniforms, as they did from other parts of the State. A few joined the Northern army, but most of our citizen soldiery favored the South. We did not attempt to carry our organizations intact into the Southern Army.

The Men Who Wore the Gray.

FATHER A. J. RYAN.

Tell it as you may,
It never can be told;
Sing it as you will
It never can be sung.
The story of the glory
Of the men who wore the gray.
In their graves so still;
The story of the living
Unforgiven, yet forgiving—
The victim still of hate,
Who have forever clung,
With a love that will not die,
To the memories of our past;
Who are patient and who wait
True and faithful to the last
For the Easter morning sky,
Where wrong's rock shall roll away
From the sepulcher of right,
And the right shall rise again
In the brightness of a light
That shall never fade away,
Triumphantly and glorious
To teach once more to men,
The conquered are victorious.
The conquered in the strife
Through their children yet shall reign
By their patience and their peace;
They shall fill the people's life,
From right's ever virgin vein,
With the purest love that flows,
Made the purer by our woes,
Without stain and without cease
Till the children of our foes
Shall be proud and glad to claim

And to write upon one scroll
Every dear and deathless name
On our Southern muster roll.
Ah! we rebels met defeat
On the gory battle field,
And we flung our muskets down,
When our bonnie flag was furled
But our right did but retreat
With pure honor for her shield,
And with justice for her crown
From the forces of the world.
(For against us thousands came,
Money brought from every clime
But we stood against them all
For the honor of our name,
Till the fated day of time
Came but to crown our fall
With a fadeless wreath of fame.)
Retreat into that shrine
Back of every Southern breast,
Your hearts my friends and mine,
Where right finds a holy rest
On the altar stairs that slope
Toward the throne where reigns the just,
Where we still live on and hope,
And in Him we place our trust.
Is it treason thus to sing?
Why then treason let it be,
Must we stoop to fawn or wrong?
To the idle must we bring
Our heart's idolatry
And the fealty of song?
No, no; the past is past,
May it never come again;
May no drum or bugle's blast,
Summon warriors to the plain.

The battle's play is o'er.
We staked our all and lost;
The red wild waves that tossed
The Southland's sacred bark
Are sleeping on the shore.
She went down in the dark;
Is it wrong for us to listen
To the waves that still will glisten
Where the wreck we loved went down?
Is it wrong to watch the willows
That are drooping o'er the grave?
Is it wrong to love our brave?
Are our memories a treason
To the powers we must obey?
Can the victors give a reason
Why the men who wore the gray
From our hearts should march away,
And should pass from us forever
Like the dreamings of the night?
Do they want the South to sever
The blood consecrated ties,
The sacred bonds of sorrow
That will link our last—tomorrow
To our glory hallowed past?
Ah! pure hearts cry, Never! never!
For each soldier heart that dies
In our memories still is beating;
Though the years are fast retreating
We remember to the last.
Nay, tell it as you may,
It never can be told;
And sing it as you will,
It never can be sung—
The story of the glory
Of our bonnie, bonnie flag,
When its battle wings were waiving

In the valley—on the crag--
On the billows of the ocean,
By the rivers' winding shore.
The years have passed away,
But, Ah! 'tis flinging still
Around our hearts to-day
The self-same spell it flung
O'er our soldiers in the gray,
Back of lines that never quailed,
Far from battle banner's flash.
There were lips that moaned and wailed,
And how many eyes that wept;
Tho' they heard no cannon crash,
Nor the terror storms of lead,
And they sighed the while they slept
When they dreamed their own were dead;
Mothers, wives and children fair,
Back of all the ranks that fought,
Knelt adown in holy prayer,
And in Heaven only sought
In their infinite despair.
Gleams of hope to light the night
Darkly gathering o'er the right.
Can a singer gather up
In the chalices of song,
Half the tears that filled the cup
Of the griefs of such a throng?
Crimson drops on battle plain,
Thro' four sorrow-laden years—
Were they richer than the rain,
That baptized our homes with tears?
Nay; no singer yet has sung
Song to tell how hearts had bled,
Where our soldiers homes among,
Wept eyes waiting for the dead.
And one statuesque, and still
(Is he in the hall to-night,

Who yet suffers for the right?)
Faithful chieftain of our cause—
Like an ocean rock his will,
Let the wild waves rise and fall;
What cares it, and what cares he?
Tho' still banned by freedom's laws,
In his home beside the sea
Lives he freest of the free.
Ah! they chained his feeble frame,
But they could not chain his thought,
Nor the right for which he fought;
And they could not chain his fame,
But they riveted his name
To the hearts of you and me.
Aged chieftian! Southern truth!
In you keeps immortal youth!
You, our truest and our best,
What care you for any ban?
Are you not the noblest guest
In the hearts of each and all?
For us all you wore wrong's chain,
And each heart is now the hall
Where you have the right to reign.
Leader of the men in gray!
Chieftian—truest of the true—
Write our story as you may,
And *you did;* but even you
With your pen could never write
Half the story of our land;
Yours the heart, and yours the hand—
Sentinels of Southern right;
Yours the brave, strong eloquence—
Your true words our last defense;
Warrior—words but even they
Failed as failed our men in gray;
Failed to tell the story grand
Of our cause and of our land.

When and Where Father Ryan Died.

The poet priest of the South, Rev. A. J. Ryan, died at St. Boniface Franciscan Convent, Louisville, Ky. What a sorrow seemed to have veiled the life and death of this sweet bard and true poet, so loved by the people of the South. There is a breath of sadness in every line of his verses, as there ever was a shade of melancholy in his face. As a prophet he thus described with wonderful accuracy his own sad last hours:

"He was dying fast and the hours went by.
　Ah! desolate hours were they;
　His mind had hidden away somewhere
　Back of a fretted and wearied brow,
　　E'er he passed from life away."

He passed from this world away on the 22d of April, at 9 p. m., 1886, at the age of forty-six. The ex-Confederates of Louisville escorted his remains to the depot. He was buried at Mobile, Ala. Few men possess the power of so withdrawing from the world around them and living in the realm of thought as he did.—Edwin Drury.

[It is a singular fact that some admirers of Father Ryan's poems believe that he is yet alive.]

I.—3

HUMOR IN CAMP.

BEN B—— was foraging, and finding a farm-house deserted, he went in to see what was lying around loose. The only thing left was the house cat. He took that back to camp. Ben said he just took it to keep the enemy from getting it.

In my regiment there was a Corporal McVay with a suit of red ringlets, and the boys would tease him about his curls. On one occasion he went on a scout. The entire scout was captured, but one of them made his escape, and he gave a most amusing account of McVay's experience with his captors. One of them insisted on having one of his curls to send to his sweetheart at home to make her think he was flirting with a red-headed little Rebel girl in Dixie. They would chaff him until he was wild and helpless with rage. It is safe to say he had his curls cut off if he ever got back to his command.

MEMORABLE EVENTS OF THE CONFEDERATE WAR.

JANUARY 5, 1861—Steamer "Star of the West" sailed from New York with supplies and re-inforcements for Fort Sumpter; arrived off

Charleston, S. C., on the 9th, was fired upon
and driven back to sea. She returned to New
York on the 12th, with two large shot holes in
her hull.

March, 1861—4th, Abraham Lincoln inaugurated President.

May, 1861—2d, Sixty-ninth New York Regiment arrived in Washington; 5th, General
Butler took possession of Relay House; 11th,
Charleston blockade established; 31st, cavalry
skirmish at Fairfax Courthouse, Va.

June, 1861—2d, battle of Phillips, Va.; Con-
federates routed; 11th, Colonel Wallace routed
Confederates at Romney, Va.; 18th, battle of
Booneville, Mo.

July, 1861—5th, President Lincoln called for
400,000 men and $400,000,000 to put down the
rebellion; battle of Carthage, Mo.; 10th, battle
of Laurel Hill; 11th, first battle of Bull Run;
Union army completely routed; 21st, second
battle of Bull Run; lasted ten hours, when panic
seized the Union army and they fled to Washington in disorder. The loss was: Confederates,
killed, 630; wounded, 2,235; missing, 150.
Union, killed, 1,011; wounded, 1,216; missing,
2,698. The numbers engaged were: Union,
65,000; Confederates in action, 47,000. This
was a terrible defeat for the Union army and a
victory for the Confederate.

August, 1861—2d, battle of Dug Spring, Mo.; 4th, battle of Athens, Mo.; 7th, Hampton, Va., burned by Confederates; 8th, battle of Wilson Creek, Mo.; Union forces, 5,200; Confederate forces, 1,500; after six hours' fighting, Confederates were repulsed; 20th, skirmish of Hawks' Nest, Va.; Confederates engaged, 4,000; Union men, 8,000; Union men routed; 28th, bombardment and capture of Forts Clark and Hatteras; Confederate loss, 765 prisoners and 1,000 stands of arms; 29th, Lexington, Mo., attacked, but repulsed with heavy loss.

September, 1861—6th, Paducah, Ky., occupied by Union forces; 10th, battle of Carnifere Ferry, Va.; 20th, Colonel Mulligan surrendered at Lexington, Mo., with 25.000 men, to the Confederates; 24th, Romney, Va., stormed and captured by Union forces.

October. 1861—3d, battle of Ball's Bluff; 21st, battle of Wild Cat, Ky.; 28th, battle of Cromwell, Ky.

November, 1861—7th. great naval fight of Hilton Head; 8th, battle of Belmont, Mo.; 11th, battle of Piketon, Ky.

December, 1861—2d, naval engagement at Newport News; 10th, shelling of Freestone Point by Union gunboats; 20th, battle of Dramsville, Mo.

January, 1862—2d, battle of Port Royal

Island, S. C.; 10th, battle of Middle Creek, Ky.; 19th, battle of Wall Spring, Ky., Confederate loss 192 killed, 68 wounded, 98 prisoners, all there were; Union loss, 39 killed, 207 wounded.

February, 1862.—6th, Fort Henry captured by Union troops; 7th and 8th, battle of Roanoke Island; Union loss, 50 killed, 222 wounded; Confederate loss, 13 killed, 39 wounded and 2,527 prisoners; 13th, battle of Fort Donelson, and captured on the 16th by Union forces; Union loss, 446 killed, 1,735 wounded, 150 prisoners; Confederate loss, 227 killed, 1,007 wounded, 13,300 prisoners; 21st, battle near Fort Craig, N. M.; Union loss, 162 killed, 40 wounded.

March, 1862—6th, 7th and 8th, battle of Pea Ridge, Ark.; Union loss, 203 killed, 972 wounded, 176 missing; Confederate loss, 1,100 killed, 2,400 wounded, 1,000 prisoners; 9th, first encounter of iron-clad vessels, Monitor and Merrimac, on the Chesapeake Bay; Confederate ship Merrimac defeated; 10th, Manassas, Va., evacuated by Confederates; 14th, battle of Newberry, N. C.; 23d, battle of Winchester, Va.; 28th, battle of Valles Ranch, N. M.

April, 1862—6th and 7th, battle of Pittsburg Landing; Union loss, 1,735 killed, 7,822 wounded, 4,044 missing; 8th and 9th, battle of Perryville, Mo.; 15th, heavy fight between Lexington and Richmond, Ky.; 18th, Gen. J. H. Morgan dashes into Lexington and captures 125 prisoners; 22d, battle of Marysville, Ark.

May, 1862—1st, New Orleans captured by Union fleets; 5th, battle of Williams, Va.; 8th, battle of West Point, Va.; 10th, surrender of Norfolk, Va.; Gen. Butler captured $800,000 in gold at New Orleans; 23d. battle of Front Royal, Va.; 25th, battle of Winchester, Va.; 27th, battle of Corinth, Miss.; 31st, battle of Fair Oaks, Va., and battle of Seven Pines, Va.

June, 1862—4th, battle of Panther Creek, N. C.; 6th, great gunboat fight before Memphis, Tenn., at the close of which Memphis surrendered to the Union army unconditionally; 8th, battle of Cross Keys, Va.; 9th, battle of Port Republic, Va.; 26th, battle of Mechanicsville, Va.; 27th, bombardment of Vicksburg, Miss.; 30th, battle of White Oak Swamp.

July, 1862—1st, battle of Malvean Hill, the last of the great seven days' battle before Richmond; total Union loss was 16,224, of which 1.565 were killed; no account of the Confederate losses; President Lincoln seemed to be alarmed and called for 600,000 more men; 5th, bombardment of Vicksburg, Miss.; 17th, postage stamps made a legal tender; 20th. Gen. J. H. Morgan and forces overtaken and scattered.

August, 1862—4th, President Lincoln ordered

300,000 more men to be drafted; 5th, battle of Baton Rouge, La.; attack on Fort Donnelson, Tenn.; 9th, battle of Cedar Mountain; 21st, five Confederate regiments crossed the Rappahannock and almost walked into the masked batteries of General Seigel, which opened fire on them of grape and canister, mowing them down by scores, 700 being killed and 2,000 captured; great mistake; battle near Centerville, Mo.; Union forces evacuated Fredericksburg, Va.; 29th, battle of Groveton, near Bull Run, Va.; 30th, Groveton battle renewed; General Pope defeated; Battle near Richmond, Ky.; Union forces defeated: 200 killed, 700 wounded and 2,000 taken prisoners.

September, 1862— —, battle near Chantilly, Va.; battle at Britton Lane, Tenn.; 12th, Harper's Ferry invested by Confederates; 14th, battle of South Mountain, Md.; Union loss, 2,325; 15th, Harper's Ferry surrendered and 11,500 Union forces prisoners; 17th, battle of Antietam; each army numbered about 100,000; losses were heavy on each side; Munfordsville, Ky., surrendered to Confederates; 4,600 prisoners; 20th, battle of Iuka, Miss.; 22d, Emancipation proclamation issued by President Lincoln.

October, 1862—3d, battle of Corinth, Miss.; Union loss 2,359, Confederate loss 9,363. Three thousand Confederates were buried on the field; it was fearful; 7th, Island No. 10, Mississippi river, surrendered after twenty-three days' bombardment; Confederate loss, 125 guns, 13 steamers, 10,000 small arms, 2,000 horses, wagons, over 6,000 prisoners; 8th and 9th, *Shiloh;* this was a famous and fearful battle; on the second day General Albert Sidney Johnston, in command of Confederates, fell on the battlefield leading a desperate charge; 11th, Pulaski surrendered after thirty hours' bombardment; 16th, battle of Camden, S. C.; 26th, Commodore Farragut demanded the surrender of New Orleans.

November, 1862—1st, Artillery fight at Philmont, Va.; 3d, reconnoissance at the base of Blue Ridge; Confederates driven into the river and many drowned; 16th, Capt. Dahlgren, with fifty-four men, dashed into Fredericksburg, Va., and surprised the Confederates; 21st, Sumner demanded the surrender of Fredericksburg, Va.; 27th, battle near Frankfort, Va.; 28th, battle of Cane Hill, Ark.

December, 1862—4th, Winchester, Va., captured by Union forces; 5th, battle near Coffeeville, Miss.; 7th, battle of Prairie Grove, Ark.; 11th, Fredericksburg, Va., shelled by Union forces; 12th, Fredericksburg captured; 13th, battle of Fredericksburg, Va.; 29th, General

Sherman repulsed by the Confederates; 31st, battle of Murfreesboro.

PAT and Mike, two brave Confederates, who had been attached in times of peace, were inseparable. One day, passing a coal shaft, Pat fell into the dark pit. Mike was deeply grieved, and called out: "Pat, if you are not dead, speak to me." Pat replied? " I am not dead, but sp'achless."

I overheard a lively discussion at Winchester, Va., when "Old Stonewall" captured it in May, 1862, from "Quartermaster" Banks, between a Federal Colonel, who was a prisoner, and a private soldier in the Thirteenth Virginia Regiment.

After the discussion had progressed for some time, the Colonel, with a considerable air of confidence, said to "Johnny:"

"I will settle the discussion, sir, by asking you just one question: '*Who fired the first gun in this war?*'"

As quick as a flash, the Confederate replied:

"*John Brown, at Harper's Ferry, sir. He fired the first gun. And Mr. Lincoln, in attempting to re-enforce Sumpter, fired the second gun. And the*

Confederates have acted upon the defensive all the time. We did not invade your country; but you invaded ours. You go home and attend to your business, and leave us to attend ours, and the war will close at once.''

The Banner Song.

By James B. Marshall.

Up, Up! with the banner, the foe is before us!
  His bayonets bristle; his sword is unsheathed.
Charge, charge! on his line with harmonious chorus,
  For the prayers go with us that beauty hath breathed.

He fights for power, for despot and plunder,
  While we are defending our altars and homes.
He has riven the firmly-knit Union asunder,
  And to bind it with tyranny's fetters, he comes.

Like the Prophet Mokanna, whose veil so resplendent,
  His monstrous deformity closely concealed,
Duplicity marks Lincoln's course, and dependent
  On falsehood is every fair promise revealed.

When that veil shall be raised, freedom's last feast be taken,
  A banquet to which all his followers will crowd,
Oh, horror of horrors! who can view it unshaken.
  Without feeling we sit—all as suppliants bowed.

We do not forget, that they once were our brothers;
  That we sat in our boyhood around the same board;
That our hearts best idolatry blest the same mothers,
  And to the same fathers libations were poured.

We rallied around the same star-spangled standard,
  When called to the field by the tocsin of war,
But they from our side have unfeelingly wandered,
  And we strip from our flag every recusant star.

They have forced us to stand by our own constitution;
  To defend our loved homesteads, our altars and fires,
While they tamely submit to a tyrant's pollution,
  Beneath whose foul tread their freedom expires.

Then up with the banner! its broad stripes wide flowing;
  'Tis the emblem of liberty—the flag of the free.
Let it wave us to triumph; and every heart glowing,
  Nerve each arm's bravest blow for our loved Tennessee.

SOUTHERN GIRLS' SONG.

AIR, "BONNIE BLUE FLAG."

Oh! yes, I am a Southern girl, I glory in the name
And boast it with far greater pride than glittering wealth
    or fame.
I envy not the Northern girl her robes of beauty rare,
Though diamonds grace her snowy neck or pearls bedeck
    her hair.

  CHORUS—Hurrah! hurrah for the Sunny South so dear,
      Three cheers for the homespun dress that South-
      ern ladies wear!

This homespun dress is plain I know—the hat quite com-
    mon, too,
But then it proves what Southern girls for Southern rights
    can do.
We've sent the bravest of our land to battle with the foe,
For we would lend a helping hand—we love the South you
    know.

CHORUS—

A soldier lad is the lad for me—a brave heart I adore,
And when the Sunny South is free, and fighting is no more,
I'll choose me then a lover brave from out that gallant band,
And the soldier lad I love the best shall have my heart and
    hand.

CHORUS—

And now, young men, one word to you; if you would win
    the fair,
Go to the field where honor calls and win your lady there;
Remember that our brightest smiles are for the true and
    brave,
And that our tears will fall for one who fills a soldier's
    grave.

CHORUS—

THE "Alabama" for some weeks played a game of hide and seek with the Federal Cruiser "Vanderbilt." When the latter would be in Simon's Bay, the former would have business in Table Bay. The Cape Town people say that the Commander of the Vanderbilt did not want to engage the Alabama from a feeling of sympathy for bold Semmes. This mystery has never been explained.

The Old Coat of Gray.

It lies there alone, it is rusted and faded,
  With a patch in the elbow, a hole in the side;
But we think of the brave boy who wore it, and ever
  Look on it with pleasure and touch it with pride.
A history clings to it over and over,
  We see a proud youth hurried off to the fray,
With his form like the oak, and his eye like the eagle's,
  How gallant he rode in the ranks of " The Gray."

It is rough, it is worn, it is tattered in places,
  But I love it the more for the story it bears—
A story of courage in struggle with sorrows,
  And a heart that bore bravely its burden of cares.
It is ragged and rusty, but ah! it was shining
  In the silkiest sheen when he wore it away,
And his smile was as bright as the glad summer morning
  When he sprang to his place in the ranks of " The Gray."

There's a rip in the sleeve and the collar is tarnished,
  The buttons all gone with their glitter and gold;
'Tis a thing of the past, and we reverently lay it
  Away with the treasures and relics of old
As the gifts of a love, solemn, sweet and unspoken
  Are cherished as leaves from a long vanished day;
We will keep the old jacket for the sake of the loved one
  Who rode in the van in the ranks of " The Gray."

Shot through with a bullet, right here in the shoulder,
  And down there the pocket is splintered and soiled.
Ah! more, see the lining is stained and discolored,
  Yes; blood drops the texture have stiffened and spoiled,
It came when he rode at the head of the column
  Charging down in the battle one deadliest day
When the squadrons of foemen were broken assunder,
  And victory rode with the ranks of " The Gray."

Its memory is sweetened and sorrow commingled,
  To me it is precious, more precious than gold;

In the rent and shot-shells a volumn is written,
  In the stains on the lining is agony told
That was ten years ago, when in life's summer morning
  He rode with his comrades into the fray;
And the old coat he wore, and the good sword he wielded
  Were all that came back from the ranks of "The Gray."

And it lies there alone, I will reverence it ever
  The patch on the elbow, the hole in the side,
For a gallanter heart never breathed than the loved one
  Who wore it in honor and soldierly pride;
Let me brush off the dust from its tatters and tarnish,
  Let me fold it up closely and lay it away—
It is all that is left of the loved and the lost one
  Who fought for the right in the ranks of "The Gray."

HISTORICAL CURIOSITY.

IT is a singular fact that a complete outline history of the Confederacy is embraced in the names of all the States composing it, to-wit: Alabama, Arkansas, Florida, Georgia, Kentucky, Louisiana, Mississippi. Missouri, North Carolina, South Carolina, Tennessee, Texas and Virginia, and is obtained in the following manner:

NATIONAL TITLE.

Confederate States of America.

CAPITAL.

Richmond, Va.

GOVERNMENT INSTITUTED.

February Eighteen, Eighteen Sixty-One.

ADMINISTRATION.

Davis, President; Stephens, Vice-President;
Hunter, Secretary; Memminger, Treasurer.

EMBASSADORS.

Mason, Slidell.

ARMY.

Confederate States Army.

NAVY.

Confederate States Navy.

ENSIGNS.

Stars and Bars, the Starry Cross.

CAUSES OF THE WAR COMBINED.

National Interference in States' Rights.

WHEN THE WAR COMMENCED.

April Fourteenth, Eighteen Sixty-One.

WHERE THE WAR COMMENCED.

Fort Sumter, South Carolina.

THREE LEADING GENERALS.

Lee, Beauregard, A. P. Hill.

THREE GREAT BATTLES OF THE WAR.

Manassas, Gettysburg, Shiloh.

THREE LEADING NAVAL OFFICERS.

Semmes, Buchanan, Mitchell.

THREE BEST NAVAL VESSELS.

Merrimac, Alabama, Arkansas.

THREE DISTINGUISHED NAVAL ACTIONS.

Hampton Roads, Cherbourg, Galveston.

THREE NOTED SIEGES.
Vicksburg, Port Hudson, Lexington.

THREE DESTRUCTIVE BOMBARDMENTS
Charleston, Mobile, Saint Phillip.

THREE DISTINGUISHED PRIVATE SOLDIERS.
Chestnut, Pelham, Mumford.

THREE STATE CAPITALS NOT CAPTURED DURING THE WAR.
Tallahassee. Fla.; Austin, Texas; Montgomery, Ala.

THREE OF THE OLDEST SOUTHERN NEWSPAPERS NOT SUPPRESSED DURING THE WAR.
Mercury (Charleston), *Examiner* (Richmond), *Register* (Mobile.)

WHEN THE WAR CLOSED.
April Ninth, Eighteen Sixty-Five.

WHERE THE WAR CLOSED.
Appomattox, Va.

War and peace are met togother,
Gray and Blue salute each other.

J. PHIN WILSON.
Paducah, (Ky.) Vol. C. S. A.

GENERAL BEAUREGARD'S WILL.

"I give to the city of Charleston, S. C., if acceptable to it, the sword which was presented to

me by the ladies of New Orleans in 1861, for the capture of Fort Sumter."

The city council of Charleston sent a committee to New Orleans for the sword, and when they returned it was formally presented to the citizens by the mayor at a large public meeting. All the survivors, the militia, bearing draped flags, the mayor and aldermen, brought it to the hall where the citizens were assembled. Church bells were tolled and cannons fired.

The Southern Cross.

A. S. MORTON, ST. PAUL, MINNESOTA.

Freedom's blazing constellation
Welcomed by the acclamation
Of a giant infant nation,
  Rose the Southern Cross.

Aye, to keep it where they found it
In the heavens!   Ne'er to ground it,
Swore ten thousand madly 'round it—
  'Round the Southern Cross."

And our hopes grew higher, higher,
For the end seemed drawing nigher,
When, above Manassas' fire,
  Waved the Southern Cross.

Matchless chiefs (a world admiring),
Wondrous deed of valor firing,

'Neath its blazing light inspiring,
  Led the Southern Cross.

And our hopes grew higher, higher,
For the end seemed drawing nigher,
When, above Manassas' fire,
  Waved the Southern Cross.

'Mid the battle's lurid glaring,
Where the torch of war was flaring;
Everywhere were deeds of daring—
  Gleamed the Southern Cross.

And the Northern heavens paling,
While the stoutest of them, quailing,
Watched in terror unavailing—
  Shone the Southern Cross.

O'er the dead and with the dying,
In the face of foemen flying,
"Down for aye with tyrants!" crying—
  Swept the Southern Cross.

Heroes bore it, proud to wave it,
Glad to give their blood to lave it,
Trusty swords were bared to save it—
  Save the Southern Cross.

Gallant lads their faith defending,
Careless of the faith impending,
Sank to rest with angels tending—
  'Neath the Southern Cross.

Lost was all for which we'd striven.
Like a bolt from heaven driven,
Like the oak by lightning riven,
  Fell the Southern Cross.

Ages hence will tell the story,
How, tho' tattered, torn and gory,
In a sea of blazing glory,
  Set the Southern Cross.

A Faithful Servant.

At the battle of Chicahominy, when General Rhodes' brigade had driven the enemy from their redoubts, and had captured the guns, the General was wounded in the arm, but would not leave the field, or make known his injury to his troops. Becoming weak, he espied an Arkansas negro, named Archie, manfully fighting behind his master, and ordered him to bring him water from a distant well. Mounting a horse, Archie dashed off to the well under a shower of bullets, and soon returned. The regiment to which he was attached (Twelfth Mississippi) was soon afterward ordered to occupy one of the captured redoubts, and to hold it at all hazards. Some of the companies being in want of ammunition, Archie again volunteered his services, and under a murderous fire went fully one mile to the rear and returned to the redoubts loaded down with haversacks filled with cartridges. This noble deed was rewarded with hearty cheers from the whole brigade.

THE BONNIE BLUE FLAG.

HARRY MACARTHY.

We are a band of brothers, and native to the soil—
Fighting for our property, we gained by honest toil;
And when our rights were threatened, the cry rose near
    and far.
Hurrah for the Bonnie Blue Flag, that bears a single star.
Hurrah! Hurrah! for Southern rights, hurrah!
Hurrah for the Bonnie Blue Flag that bears a single star.

As long as the Union was faithful to her trust,
Like friends and like brothers, kind we were and just,
But now, when Northern treachery attempts our rights to
    mar,
We hoist on high the Bonnie Blue Flag, that bears a single
    star.

    [CHORUS—Hurrah! etc.]

First, gallant South Carolina nobly made the stand;
Then came Alabama, and took her by the hand.
Next, quickly Mississippi, Georgia and Florida,
All raised on high the Bonnie Blue Flag, that bears a single
    star.

    [CHORUS—Hurrah! hurrah! etc. |

Ye men of valor, gather 'round the banner of the right—
Texas and fair Louisiana shall join us in the fight.
Davis, our loved President, and Stephens, statesman rare,
Now rally 'round the Bonnie Blue Flag, that bears a single
    star.

    [CHORUS—Hurrah! hurrah!]

And here's to brave Virginia, the Old Dominion State,
With the young Confederacy at length has joined her fate.
Impelled by her example, now other States prepare
To hoist on high the Bonnie Blue Flag that bears a single
    star.

    [CHORUS - Hurrah! hurrah! |

Then, here's to the Confederacy—strong we are and brave.
Like patriots of old, we fight our heiritage to save,
And rather than submit to shame, to die we would prefer.
So cheer for the Bonnie Blue Flag that bears a single star.

[CHORUS—Hurrah! hurrah!]

Then cheer, boys, cheer!   Raise the joyous shout.
Arkansas and North Carolina now have both gone out;
And let another rousing cheer for Tennessee be given;
The single star of the Bonnie Blue Flag has grown to be
  eleven.
Hurrah for Southern rights, hurrah!
Hurrah! for the Bonnie Blue Flag has gained the eleventh
  star!

THE MULE BALKED.

OUR regiment was in camp at Harper's Ferry.
and one bright morning a comrade and I se-
cured permission to visit a farm house some distance away where we knew there was some
poultry. We rode horses and had some money
in our pockets to purchase the chickens and
turkeys—for on this occasion we had made up
our minds to forego foraging, but later circumstances arose that made it necessary to forget
our good resolutions. Turning our horses into
a grass field near the house, we left them to
graze at will. We met the farmer on an old-

fashioned porch that ran the whole front of the quaint farm house. I told the farmer we had come to try some of his poultry, at which his Southern blood began to boil. He swore he would rather see every chicken and turkey rot before he would sell to any blamed Yankee for a thousand times their worth. That settled it with us. Our Northern blood had reached fire heat. We could not stand such an insult, and went straightway to the barn, where a fine lot of fowls were pecking grain. It did not take us long to tie the legs of a goodly number of chickens and turkeys. As I was in the act of tying up the legs of a proud gobbler, I looked up, and to my dismay saw coming up the lane a small company of Confederate cavalry. I took in the situation at a glance. I knew we had not time to reach our horses, and to escape on foot was impossible. In the barn-yard were two fine sleek mules. Throwing my string of fowls over the back of one, and jumping astride the animal, I shouted to " Bill." my comrade, to follow my example. He did so, and I took the lead for the camp. The mule I was on had taken but a few jumps, when I heard " Bill " shout, " Holy smoke! he's balked, Jim." The Johnnies were close at hand. I shouted back, " Crawl on his neck Bill, and chaw his ear!" Bill lost no time in trying the experiment. He got the end of the animal's long ear into his mouth and began operations. The mule gave a squeal like that of a stuck pig, and rushed madly after its mate; I was riding for dear life. Suddenly I saw something loom up and rush past me. It was "Bill" and his mule. Bill's teeth were imbedded in the animal's ear and blood trickled down the side of its head. Bill was all humped upon his mad steed and presented a most ludicrous sight. The turkeys flopped their wings and the chickens made a terrible clatter, which only served to make the mule go faster. I heard the Johnnie's behind us laugh. They fired at us, but we were not hit. I am sure they could not have hit "Bill." Through the picket line of our regiment and on through the camp went "Bill's" mule, the fowls bobbing up and down at every jump. I gathered all my lung powers and shouted, "Let go the mule's ear Bill, we are safe." Bill heard me and let go; he finally stopped the mule; he had chewed off half his ear. Bill allowed it was the toughest bit of meat he had ever tackled, but that night he got square on roast turkey and chicken. We lost two of the best horses in our army.

History of Postage Stamps Used in the Confederate States of America.

South Carolina seceded December 20, 1860, and was quickly followed by Mississippi, Alabama, Florida, Georgia and Louisiana. Jefferson Davis was elected President, and was inaugurated at Montgomery, Ala., February 18, 1861. Up to the firing on Fort Sumter (April 11), the postal affairs seem to have been carried on with fair regularity. Letters continued to be mailed throughout the South, bearing United States stamps, during the first few months of 1861, but the supply of these stamps was soon exhausted, and most of the postmasters were soon unable to furnish stamps or envelopes. To those situated in small towns this made but little difference. but in commercial centers much inconvenience was realized. An agent of a prominent bank note company of New York City was in Montgomery, Ala., in February, 1861, for the purpose of making a contract to supply stamps to the new government, but the bombardment of Fort Sumter made it evident that goods could not be delivered, and negotiations were discontinued. The Confederate government succeeded, however, in buying a large quanity of paper in New York City. which was forwarded to Louisville. Ky., and from there run through to Montgomery, Ala. This paper was afterward used for the manufacture of stamps issued by the general government. On the 11th of March, 1861, the permanent constitution was adopted by Congress, and in it was a clause providing that the postoffice department must pay its own expenses, from its own resources, after the 1st day of March, 1863. The postoffice department was at once organized with John H. Reagan as postmaster-general, but its chief work devolved upon H. St. George Offutt, who, from his long connection with the postoffice department. was eminently fitted to perform the difficult task. Mr. Offutt occupied the position of chief clerk of the auditor's office at the secession of South Carolina, but relinquished that position to join the Confederate army, although his native State (Missouri) did not leave the Union. The valuable library of postal works (the only complete one in the United States) which he took with him must have been of incalculable benefit in starting such a complicated machine as a post-office department for a large country. However. on the 1st of June, 1861, we find the department prepared with every thing necessary for the successful operation of the offices contained within its territory.

The following gentlemen occupied the principal positions in the new department: John H.

Reagan, postmaster-general; B. Fuller, chief clerk; H. St. G. Offutt, chief of the contract bureau; J. L. Harrell, chief of finance bureau; B. N. Clements, chief of appointment bureau; Bolling Baker, auditor. Most of the old United States postmasters were retained on their taking the oath of allegiance to the Confederate States, and in one case at least a competent man was allowed to keep his post without taking the prescribed oath. The few Union men who held office at the South were compelled to retain their office until new appointments could be made. A majority of the postmasters remitted the full amount due the United States postoffice department up the 31st of June, and returned all the stamps and postoffice property that was in their charge. Others either kept the property or turned it over to the Confederate department.

Subsequently the department issued a circular ordering all postmasters to send all United States property, stamps, etc., to Richmond, where they were utilized in various ways; but this was not until after the war began. Many of the most enterprising postmasters in the South asked and obtained permission to issue stamps pending the preparation of those by the Confederate government. Probably some of the postmasters of the smaller towns issued stamps and stamped envelopes on their own responsibility. The following letters will show how and why postmasters were obliged to make these stamps:

"DEAR SIR—In reply to your note of the 12th inst., I would say that the stamps you inclosed me were got up by me here in Memphis. When Tennessee passed the ordinance of secession the old government stamps were worthless, and, as I found it impossible to get along without stamps, I asked and procured the consent of the government at Richmond to get up temporary stamps until the postmaster-general could furnish me with regular stamps. Those you inclosed me were in use several months, and were the only ones used. A stamp was shortly afterward manufactured at Richmond, after which those issued were taken in and destroyed.

"M. C. GALLOWAY.

"Memphis, July 17."

The general government issued the first Confederate postage stamps on October 18th, 1861, a 5-cent green stamp. This was soon followed by the 10-cent blue stamp, the 2-cent green stamp, and, the green ink being exhausted, printed in blue and in red. All these stamps were prepared by Messrs. Hoyen & Ludwig, of Richmond, Va. Later on Messrs. De La Rue & Co. prepared the plates and furnished the stamps of the 5-cent blue and a 1-cent orange, which was never used. The plates of the 5-cent blue were afterward used by Messrs. Archer & Daly in printing the regular supply. They furnished also the 10-cent blue stamp, three varieties, and the 20-cent green. A short time after the first 10-cent blue stamp was issued, President Davis met Colonel Offut and asked him if he remembered A. W. Brown's objection to the portrait. Upon an affirmative answer being given, the President remarked: "I was walking across the park to-day, on my way to my office, when I met a tall North Carolina soldier, who accosted me: 'Is your name Davis?' 'Yes.' 'President Davis?' 'Yes.' 'I thought so, you look so much like a postage stamp.'" In addition to their use as postage stamps, they were used as small change by the soldiers and citizens, just as United States postage stamps were sent through the lines by special arrangement between the United States of America and the Confederate States of America. The following notice is a sample:

To Those Who Wish to Send Letters North:

HEADQUARTERS, DEPARTMENT OF NORFOLK.

NORFOLK, January 9, 1862·

Person wishing to send letters to the United States will observe the following directions:

1. Letters must have on the envelope, in addition to the address of the person to whom they are intended, " Via Norfolk and Flag of Truce."

2. Write no more than one page.
3. Enclose money to pay the United States postage.
4. Do not address letters to Gen. Huger.

BENJ. HUGER, JR.,
First Lieutenant and V. D. C.

In May, 1865, the plates, stamps, archives, etc., were surrendered to the United States authorities at Chester, S. C., and were probably transferred to Washington. The full history of the Post-Office Department of the Confederate States cannot be written until these archives are open for examination.

Six months elapsed between the firing on Fort Sumter (April 11, 1861), and the issue of the stamps by the general government (October 18, 1861), and the mails were transferred regularly. Many millions of letters were forwarded during that time. The bulk of these were probably destroyed at the time, but there must still be in existence an enormous quantity of letters bearing the stamps used at that period.

THE following oath was administered to the members of a volunteer company during the war:

"You solemnly swear to obey, fight for and maintain the laws of the Confederate government and Constitution, and support John W. Dean for Captain of this company."

Upon inquiry it was learned that the reason the last clause was inserted, was because he had been quite active in getting up a company before, and when they elected their officers he was left out. and he wanted to make sure.

Gubernatorial Confederates.

David P. Lewis (signer of Confederate Constitution), Governor of Alabama 1872–74.

Williamson R. W. Cobb, member of Confederate Congress), Governor of Alabama 1878–82.

Edward A. O'Neal (Brigadier General). Governor of Alabama 1882–86.

Augustus H. Garland (member of both houses of Confederate Congress). Governor of Arkansas 1875–77.

T. J. Churchill (Brigadier General), Governor of Arkansas 1881–83.

Edward A. Perry (Brigadier General), Governor of Florida 1885–89.

Charles J. Jenkins (State Supreme Court, Judge of Georgia during Confederacy), Governor of Georgia 1865–68.

Rufus B. Bullock (Acting Assistant Quarter-master-General.)

James M. Smith (member of Confederate Congress), Governor of Georgia 1872–76.

Alexander H. Stephens (Vice-President), Governor of Georgia 1882–83.

John B. Gordon (Lieutenant General), Governor of Georgia 1886–90.

Alfred H. Colquitt (Brigadier General), Governor of Georgia 1876–82.

Simon B. Buckner (Lieutenant General). Governor of Kentucky 1887–91.

Francis T. Nichols (Brigadier General). Governor of Louisiana 1877–80, 1888–92.

Benjamin G. Humphreys (Brigadier General). Governor of Mississippi 1865–68.

James L. Alcorn (Brigadier General of Mississippi State troops during Confederacy). Governor of Mississippi 1869–71.

Robert Lowery (Brigadier General), Governor of Mississippi, 1882–90.

John S. Marmaduke (Major General). Governor of Missouri 1885–87.

Zebulon B. Vance ("War Governor"), Governor of North Carolina 1877–79.

Alfred M. Scales (Brigadier General). Governor of North Carolina 1885–89.

Benjamin F. Perry (Confederate District Judge), Governor of South Carolina 1865–66.

James L. Orr (member of Confederate senate), Governor of South Carolina 1866–69.

Wade Hampton (Lieutenant General), Governor of South Carolina 1876–78.

William D. Sempson (member of Confederate Congress), Governor of South Carolina 1878–80.

Johnson Hagood (Brigadier General), Governor of South Carolina 1880–82.

John C. Brown (Major General), Governor of Tennessee 1871–75.

William B. Bate (Major General), Governer of Tennessee 1883–87.

James W. Throckmorton (Brigadier General of Texas State troops), Governor of Texas 1866–91.

James L. Kemper (Major General), Governor of Virginia 1874–78.

Lawrence S. Ross (Brigadier General), Governor of Texas 1887–91.

F. W. M. Holliday (member of Confederate congress), Governor of Virginia 1878–82.

Fitzhugh Lee (Major General), Governor of Virginia 1886–90.

Names of other governors who were Confederate officers:

Governor Thomas Seay, who was governor of Alabama 1886–90.

Governor Cameron.

Governor McKinney.

Governor O'Ferrall.

Gov. Stone, of Mississippi.

James S. Boyton, Governor of Georgia 1883.

Henry McDaniel (Major), 1883.

W. J. Northen, Governor 1890–94.

Col. Peter Richardson, Governor South Carolina 1886.

Carter L. Stevenson, Governor West Virginia 1877–81.

James P. McCreary.

Luke P. Blackburn.

OH, HE'S NOTHING BUT A SOLDIER.

BY A YOUNG REBEL ESQUIRE.   (Air: "Annie Laurie.")

Oh, he's nothing but a soldier,
  But he's coming here to-night,
For I saw him pass this morning,
  With his uniform so bright.
He was coming in from picket.
  Whilst he sang a sweet refrain,
And he kissed his hand to some one
  Peering through the window-pane.

Ah! he rode no dashing charger,
  "With a black and flowing mane,"
But his bayonet glistened brightly
  As the sun lit up the plain.
No waving plume or feather,
  Flashed its crimson in the light.
He belongs to the light infantry,
  And he came to the war to fight.

I.—5

Oh! he's nothing but a soldier;
  His trust is in his sword—
To carve his way to glory
  Through the servile Yankee horde.
No pompous pageant heralds him,
  No sycophants attend.
In his belt you see his body guard,
  His tried and trusty friend.

Oh! he's nothing but a soldier,
  And a stranger in our land.
His home is in the Sunny South,
  By the blue gulf's golden strand.
But I wish I knew his people—
  Some little of his past—
For father's always telling me
  About our *social caste.*

Oh! he's nothing but a soldier,
  But his eyes are very fine,
And I some times think, when passing,
  They are piercing into mine.
Pshaw, he's nothing but a soldier;
  Come, let me be discreet;
But really, for a soldier,
  His toilet 's very neat.

Oh! he's nothing but a soldier;
  But last night he came to tea—
What an interesting soldier—
  But then he's rather free;
'Twas 2 o'clock this morning
  Before he took his leave.
He has my ring—the fellow—
  But what's the use to grieve.

He has been again to see us—
  This gentleman in gray.
He calls to see us often—

Our house is on his way.
At times he sadly seeks the shade
  Of yonder grove of trees.
I watched him once—this soldier—
  I saw him on his knees.

One day last week I asked him
  To tell me of his home.
He answered, pointing to his camp,
  "Where'er these brave ones roam."
I asked him once to tell me
  Of his mother, sisters, dear.
A funeral cortege passed along—
  Said he: "You have them here."

Oh! he's nothing but a soldier,
  But this I know right well:
He has a heart of softness,
  Where tender virtues dwell;
For once when we were talking,
  And no one else was near,
I saw him very plainly
  Try to hide a starting tear.

We were speaking of Manassas—
  That first great bloody day,
When a handful of our brave ones
  Held the Yankee hosts at bay.
'Twas here he lost his aged sire,
  While fighting by his side.
He sleeps beneath the crimson turf
  Where rolled that bloody tide.

Oh! he's nothing but a soldier,
  But within that eye so clear
There lurks no craven spirit—
  No timid glance of fear.
For though, at pity's pleading,
  It can melt with tender light,

I've seen it flash like lightning
  Across the brow of night.

Oh! he's nothing but a soldier,
  Such as pass us every day.
He calls them "ragged rebels,"
  But, you know, that's just his way.
But there's one thing very funny—
  One thing I can't explain—
That when this soldier goes away,
  I wish him back again.

Oh! he's nothing but a soldier—
  A stranger yet to fame.
But they tell me in the army
  That the "boys" all know his name.
The Yankees, too, have heard it.
  They dread his battle shout;
They have no wish to meet him—
  This dreaded Southern scout.

Oh! he's nothing but a soldier,
  Yet, you'd call his features good.
That *cut* he got at West Point,
  While fighting under Hood.
He has a halting in his gait—
  A trifle in the knee—
He brought it back from Sharpsburg,
  Where he went with General Lee.

Oh! he's nothing but a soldier,
  But his triumphs are not few.
He has seen our glorious battle-flag,
  In all its trials through.
At Seven Pines he followed it—
  On the fights at Gaines' Mill,
At Williamsburg, at West Point,
  In the smoke at Malvern Hill.

Oh! he's nothing but a soldier,
  But then its very queer,
I feel somehow, when absent,
  I'd rather have him near.
He's gone to meet the foeman—
  To stay the bloody track.
Oh! Heaven shield the soldier!
  Oh! God, *let him* come back!

    *   *   *   *

He is back again—the soldier—
  With his eyes so deep and clear,
And his voice, like falling waters,
  Maketh music to my ear.
One empty coat-sleeve dangles
  Where once a stout arm grew,
But the soldier says in "hugging"
  He has no use for two.

Oh! he's nothing but a soldier,
  And I know that on his form
He bears the scars of conflict
  Of many a battle storm,
But I wouldn't give this soldier,
  In his simple, humble home,
For all your useless "dandies"
  That strut about the town.

    *   *   *   *

He's back again—this soldier—
  He's sitting by my side.
To-morrow, "Ho! for Texas!"
  With his young Virginia bride.
True, he's nothing but a soldier,
  But I'm now his loving wife,
Pledged, through good report or evil,
  To dwell with him through life.

The Boy Soldier.

During the battle of Chancellorville a Confederate major met a lad returning from the front. His arm, held by shreds of flesh, was dangling from the elbow. "Mister," said the boy to the officer, "can't you cut this thing off? It keeps knocking against the trees, and it's might'ly in my way." The major dismounted, cut off the useless limb, and tied a strap of his blouse around the stump to stop the bleeding. "What regiment do you belong to?" he asked his thankful patient. "I belong to that North Carolina regiment in there," answered the lad, pointing to where the battle was raging. "I am just sixteen, and this is my first fight. Don't you think it was hard I should get hit the first time I ever was in battle? We drove them out of the line of breastworks, and I was on top of the second when I got hit."

My Warrior Boy.

Thou hast gone forth, my darling one,
  To battle with the brave,
To strike in Freedom's sacred cause,
  Or win an early grave.
With vet'rans grim and stalwart men
  Thy pathway lieth now,

Though fifteen summers scarce have shed
  Their blossoms on thy brow.

My babe in years, my warrior boy!
  Oh, if a mother's tears
Could call thee back to be my joy
  And still these anxious fears,
I'd dash the traitor drops away,
  That would unnerve thy hand,
Now raised to strike in freedom's cause
  For thy dear native land!

God speed thee on thy course, my boy,
  Where'er thy pathway lie,
And guard thee when the leaden hail
  Shall thick around thee fly.
But when our sacred cause is won
  And peace again shall reign,
Come back to me, my darling son,
  And light my life again.

At the commencement of the year 1861 there were, on the Northern coast, one vessel, and forty-two in the United States navy. At the close of the year there were 264.

BATTLES IN TRANS-MISSISSIPPI DEPARTMENT.

J. A. MATHES, SENECA, MO.

At the battle of Wilson's Creek the Federals were completely routed. They left General Lyons dead on the field, lying in the hot sun, with a handkerchief over his face. Bailey Armstrong and comrade, Arch Sevier, discovered him. Sevier was acquainted with General Lyons in St. Louis. and, seeing the epaulets, he raised the handkerchief and recognized him. He and Armstrong carried him to the shade.

Our cavalry followed the enemy to the railroad at Rolla, about fifty or seventy-five miles away, capturing many of them. They lost two to our one at Wilson's Creek, although not more than two-thirds of us were armed.

We were not whipped at all at Pea Ridge· R. M. Johnson, my Captain. heard Gen. Price ask Gen. Van Dorn for two hours in which to rout them, but Van Dorn ordered him to fall back. Gen. Price turned his horse with tears in his eyes.

At Prairie Grove we whipped the enemy from early morn until dark, driving them from every position. We killed and wounded as many again as they did of us; yet at midnight we were ordered to march by daylight when we retreated again. One-third of the army would go no further south. as they could see nothing to run from.

If we could have had "Pap" Price in command this side of the river there would be a different tale to tell.

Quantrell's Call.

Air, Pirate's Serenade.

Up, comrades up, the moon is in the west,
  And we must be gone at the dawn of the day,
The hounds of old Pennoc shall find but the nest,
  For the Quantrell they seek shall be far, far away;
Their toils after us shall ever be vain,
Let them scout through the brush and scour the plain,
We'll pass through their midst in the deep of the night,
We're lions in combat, and eagles in flight.

> Chorus—Then arouse, my brave band, up, up and away,
>   Press hard on the foe at the dawn of the day;
>   Look well to your steeds, so gallant in chase;
>   They may never give o'er till they win well
>   the race.

When Pennoc is weary and the chase given o'er,
  We'll come as a thunderbolt comes in a cloud;
We'll trample, we'll rout, we'll bathe in their gore,
  We'll smite the oppressor and humble the proud.
But few shall escape us, but few shall be spared,
For keen are our sabre's which vengeance hath bared.
None are so mighty, so strong in the flight,
As our warrior's who battle for Southern rights.

> Chorus—

The brush is our homes, the green sod our bed,
Our drink from the river, and roots for our bread.
We pine not for more, we bow not the head,
For freedom is ever within the green wood.
The tyrants shan't conquer, the fetter's shan't bind,
For true are our rifles, our steeds like the wind.
We'll shield not the sword, we'll draw not the rein
'Till the Federals are banished from Missouri again.

> Chorus—

Battles and Skirmishes Fought During the Civil War.

In Pennsylvania, 2; Marryland, 17; District of Columbia, 1; Virginia, 240; West Virginia, 52; Kentucky, 46; Tennessee, 110; Missouri, 109; Arkansas, 51; South Carolina, 18; North Carolina, 32; Louisiana, 33; Mississippi, 84; Alabama, 19; Florida, 15; Ohio, 2; Indiana, 2; Illinois, 1; Texas, 4; Indian Territory, 2; Kansas, 2. Of these 842 battles and skimishes, 107 were important battles, while many of the others were slight collisions of no great consequence. The two each reported in Ohio and Indiana were due to John Morgan's raid. It will easily be seen that Virginia was the battle-field of the war.

[Total number of men called for in the Union army was 2,942,788, and the total number furnished was 2,690,401.]

The Jacket of Gray.

Mrs. C. A. Ball.

Fold it carefully, lay it aside,
Tenderly touch it; look on it with pride,
For dear must it be to our hearts evermore,
The Jacket of Gray our loved soldier boy wore.

Can we ever forget when he joined the brave band
Who rose in defense of our dear Southern land,

And in his bright youth hurried on to the fray,
How proudly he donned it—the Jacket of Gray?

His fond mother blest him and looked up above,
Commending to Heaven the child of her love;
What anguish was her's—mortal tongue cannot say,
When he passed from her sight in the Jacket of Gray.

But her country had called, and she would not repine,
Though costly the sacrifice placed on its shrine.
Her heart's dearest hopes on its altar she lay
When she sent out her boy in his Jacket of Gray.

Months passed, war's thunder rolled over the land,
Unsheathed was the sword and lighted the brand;
We heard in the distance the sound of the fray
And prayed for our boy in the Jacket of Gray.

Ah! vain, all vain, were our prayers and our tears,
The glad shout of victory rang in our ears;
But our treasured one on the red battlefield lay
While the life blood oozed out on the Jacket of Gray.

His comrades found him, and tenderly bore
The cold, lifeless form to his home by the shore;
Oh! dark were our hearts on that terrible day
When we saw our dear boy in the Jacket of Gray.

Ah! spotted and tattered and stained now with gore
Was the garment which once he so proudly wore.
We bitterly wept as we took it away
And replaced with death's white robe the Jacket of Gray.

We laid him to rest in his cold narrow bed,
And graved on the marble we placed near his head,
As the proudest tribute our sad hearts could pay,
He never disgraced the Jacket Gray.

Then fold it up gently, lay it aside,
Tenderly touch it, look on it with pride;
For dear must it be to our hearts evermore
The Jacket of Gray our loved soldier boy wore.

Charleston, S. C

Colonel Shelby's Missouri Cavalry Brigade in Arkansas.

Thursday, the 12th of March, 1863, was a gala day for this brigade. The three regiments composing it had been for some time drilling in friendly competition and in obedience to Colonel Shelby's orders, were assembled on a trial of skill in all the intricate and difficult evolutions in company and battalion. The day was delightful—a sweet south wind had blown all the night before from the land of roses, and early spring had laid her young brow upon the roseate sky, and curled her azure hair upon the budding trees and upon the waking earth with tread as soft as angel footfalls on some velvet floor. By 10 o'clock the wide and level field selected for the purpose began to be filled, and the regiments came marching from the surrounding woods and *debouched* upon the plain with the glory and memory of Cane Hill, Prairie Grove, White Springs, Hartville—eyes kindled with a battle light, hearts throbbed high with hope, and many an anxious gaze went far away northward, where the oppressed were waiting for forms that came not, for the gleaming of mingled banners that never gladdened into full fruition. Soonest on the field came the gallant First, with Frank Gordon at its head, as when in the dread and the gloom of that tangled copse at Hartville he

led them to the charge, his best and bravest
falling all around him. Then the fighting Third,
with Thompson in advance—always cool, cautious, wary. The First presented arms, and
they halted in column for the final struggle.
Lastly came the charging Second, and with it
Jeans and Shanks—the former the grim old
fighter that even now scares the visions of Union
men in Missouri, the latter the same bold, daring, dashing, chivalrous dragoon, with

> "Red hand in the foray,
> Sage counsel in chamber."

The field was surrounded by a heavy rail fence,
with openings on one side for the various regiments and spectators to pass through. All the
youth and the beauty and bloom of Batesville,
Ark., were present; gaily caparisoned steeds
danced in the sunlight; black eyes, blue eyes,
and hazel eyes shot glances hot enough and
wild enough to stir a fever in the blood of age;
old men forgot their cares and came creeping
to the inner verge of the square and looked
with joyful faces; old ladies came to see and enjoy, clapped their hands and almost exclaimed:
"I would I were a girl again." It required but
a little stretch of the imagination to call up the
knightly days of yore, when plumes were rent
and crests were shorn, and women crowned the
manly sport with wreaths of flowers and smiles.

The bugles rang out their merry peals, the regiments sprang from listlessness to attention, and at the northern gateway a bright and beautiful cavalcade came gleaming through. Not a cloud was in the sky. Nature's old heart was rich in sympathy, and the air sweet with the blush of the coming spring.

Would it be just to particularize the ladies? Why not? Let it go forth now to the South that wherever blows fall thick and fast, wherever Greek meets Greek. there will Joe Shelby's Missouri cavalry brigade proclaim the Batesville girls the fairest of the fair, and

> "Their empire shall last
> 'Till the red flag by inches is torn from the mast."

There was Miss N. W.. the beautiful. the daring, the dashing. the fascinating "Di Vernon," with a world of meaning in her wild, black eyes. and a glance like the sunlight that flashes on steel.

There was Miss E. W., young and beautiful. with step as free as the wild gazelle. There was Miss E. B., polished as an icicle. but warm and admiring as young love's first dream, and many, many others that watched the drill of the brave soldiers. who were exiles from home; and they spoke kind words of cheer and hope, and thrilled with old memories—the men swore deeper vows, lighted sterner fires than ever yet to defend the ladies of Arkansas.

The champion companies were "A" and "C" of the First, "A" of the Twenty-first, and "A" and "K" of the Third.

The drilling now began in earnest. The companies were admirably disciplined and walked and moved in position as veterans. Finally, the contest narrowed down to "A" of the First and "K" of the Third. The prize was three days' furlough, and both companies felt their honor at stake, and struggled manfully, not so much for the prize as the credit. The judges were Colonel J. T. Cearnel, the same that led almost a forlorn hope at Elk Horn and was badly wounded; Captain W. M. Price, and General Marmaduke's adjutant, Captain G. G. Williams. The two companies drilled and drilled and the ladies admired until it was decided to dismiss them for the day, and render the verdict next morning.

Company "A," of the First Regiment, is that company of Missourians which was detained at DeValls' Bluff last summer; and, ladies of Little Rock, it is the same company that won your beautiful flag sent to Gen. Marmaduke to be given to the bravest company in the next engagement.

When the company drills were over. Col.

Shelby gave command for a grand brigade movement—squares were formed, movements *en echelon*, in column, in every way laid down in Hardee, were executed with great rapidity and skill. The spectators were delighted. Never was a command in brighter spirits—more eager for the fray.

The pageant closed at sundown with three grand dress parades, and the large crowd dispersed expressing great satisfaction at the result. The judges' decision was that of a tie between companies "A" and "R," so both obtained the furlough. And whatever of skill and proficiency company "A" has attained, it is almost due to Col. Kelly, of Gen. Parson's command. In Mississippi's sultry swamps he drilled us— that noble old Roman with eyes of fire, and words of deep but generous energy. God bless him! Many a brave heart thinks of him often, and many prayers go up that he may receive a command, proportionate to his fine intellect and military abilities.

When the warfare is over; when peace strikes records with her history; when our glorious cause shall rise beautiful from its urn of death— then let our past be written; then let the song go forth:

> "Ah! soldiers to your honored rest,
> Your youth and valor bearing;
> The bravest are the tenderest,
> The loving are the daring."

—FIRST REGIMENT.

[How beautiful the affection of a soldier for his comrade in arms, and his devotion to a brave commander.]

S. R.

BY TELEGRAPH.

FROM THE TRUE DEMOCRAT.

(Published by R. S. Yerkes & Co., Little Rock, Ark.)

HEADQUARTERS DEPARTMENT TRANS-MISSIS-
SIPPI, ALEXANDRIA, LA., March 7, 1863.

GENERAL ORDER NO. 1.

1. In conformity with instructions from the War Department, at Richmond, Va., dated February 9, 1863, the undersigned hereby assumes command of the Confederate forces west of the Mississippi.

2. Until further orders the Department headquarters are established at Alexandria, La.

E. KIRBY SMITH,
Lieutenant General Commanding.
J. F. BELTON,
A. A. General.

PORT HUDSON, March 20.

Since the first fight here the Yankees are occasionally shelling the place, but without any effect. Off sloop of war Mississippi we took thirty-two fine guns. They have been safely landed by our forces. Provisions are arriving daily.

The report of Confederate success near Woodstock, Va., is confirmed. The Federal loss in killed and wounded is considerable. We have captured 250 prisoners.

———

MOBILE, March 24.

The *Tribune* has reliable information from Pensacola, stating that the city had been evacuated by order of Banks, for the purpose of reinforcing the Mississippi river expedition. The abolitionists burned thirty or forty houses before leaving. They took all the negroes to New Orleans.

———

CHATTANOOGA, March 24.

There has been no movement of the army in Tennessee. On Friday the enemy advanced on the roads from Franklin towards Columbia, but on Saturday they returned to Franklin. Van Dorn is still on the north side of Duck river. Our forces occupy Florence and Tuscumbia, and there is no movement from Corinth in this direction. Morgan had a fight in Cannon county, Tennessee, with an overwhelming force of the enemy. He fought gallantly and killed and wounded a number of the foe. but was forced to retire before superior numbers.

———

MOBILE. March 23.

Official intelligence has been received of the evacuation of Pensacola by the enemy. They now occupy the navy yard and Forts Barrancas and Pickens. The garrison of the town and all others that could be spared have been sent to Gen. Banks. ————

CAIRO, March 25.

Later news from Vicksburg confirms the arrival of the gunboats Hartford and Albatross of Farragut's fleet at the north of the canal on the 20th. An officer from on board had arrived at Grant's headquarters bringing dispatches from Banks. Seven of Farragut's boats run the blockade at Port Hudson, but. after coming up some distance. all but two returned.

———

HEADQUARTERS DISTRICT OF WESTERN LA.,
NEAR BERWICK'S BAY. March 28. 1863.

General S. Cooper, Adjutant and Inspector General, Richmond, Va.:

I have the honor to report the capture of the Federal gunboat Diana at the Point today. She mounts five heavy guns. Boat not seriously injured, and will be immediately put into service. Enemy's loss, in killed, wounded and prisoners, 150.   Your obedient servant,

[Signed.]   R. TAYLOR,

Major General Commanding.

MONROE, April 13.

News from east of Mississippi: Banks fallen back with one division of his army at Baton Rouge; the rest of his forces have gone down the river. Great consternation in Kentucky in consequence of the advance of the Confederates in Lexington. Richardson's guerrillas fought a regiment of the enemy at Somerville, killing and wounding eighty. The New Orleans *Era* of the 22d ult. gives particulars of the capture of the Federal gunboat Diana on the Atchafalaya, by Sibley's command. Diana was commanded by Captain Peterson, and had on board Company A, 22d Connecticut, and Company F, 16th New York Regiment—in all, 120 officers, privates and sailors, all of whom fell into our hands, together with the boat, one 32-pounder rifle, parrot, two smooth-bore.

CABELL'S BRIGADE CAMP AT OZARK, ARK., }
          March 27, 1863.   }

At a meeting of the commissioned officers of this brigade, on the 27th day of March, 1863, the following proceedings were had, viz:

On motion of Colonel Scott, commanding post at Ozark, Ark., Lieutenant Colonel Lee L. Thomson, of Carroll's Regiment of Arkansas Cavalry, was called to the chair, and Lieutenant Andrew I. Quindley, of Carroll's Regiment, was made secretary.

The object of the meeting being explained by the chairman to be an expression of their sorrow at the death of their fellow officer, Major Hall S. McConnell. On motion of Captain Gordon, of Carroll's Regiment, the chairman appointed the following committee to draft suitable resolutions: Captains Gordon, Jefferson and Lieutenant Sadler, of Carroll's Regiment, and Captains Basham and Paine, of the Partisan Rangers.

In due time the committee reported the following resolutions:

On the 22d day of March, 1863, Major Hall S. McConnell, being on a scout in the vicinity of White River, in Washington County, Arkansas, learned the whereabouts of a Federal scouting party, and immediately pursued and overtook them, and, whilst gallantly charging them at the head of his command, was shot dead; therefore, be it

Resolved, While it is a fact that brave men are liable to fall in battle, it is equally true that we all sooner or later may realize the same fate. It is to be expected that many a gallant son of the South will be offered as willing sacrifices in their country's cause. To those who know him well, the loss of Major McConnell is felt to be something more than the sad casualties of the war.

Resolved, That, being deeply impressed with the solemnity of this truth, the officers of Brigadier-General Cabell's command have been called together in consequence of the common bereavement.

Resolved, That the Confederate army has lost a gallant officer and patriot, and his survivors a generous, warm-hearted friend, companion and brother.

Resolved, That we feel his mother's, brothers' and sisters' loss has been greater than ours. He "who suffereth not a sparrow to fall except for some wise and beneficient cause" will "temper the wind to the shorn lamb," and afford consolation in this hour of bereavement.

Resolved, That a copy of these resolutions be furnished to Mrs. Susan McConnell and family, at Clarksville, Ark., as a testimonial of our kind sympathies with them in their loss, which we claim to be a common loss—as well to us and the country as to them. Of our high appreciation of the son and brother as an officer and companion in arms, and to assure them that while he will be missed in the home circle, his loss has caused a sad vacuum among his messmates and friends in the army.

Resolved, That we hereby bear testimony to the great moral worth of our brother soldier, Hall S. McConnell. Whether as an officer, a private or a citizen, he was well qualified to adorn any position which he would consent to occupy.

Resolved, That the *True Democrat*, and other Arkansas papers, be requested to publish the foregoing.

The resolutions were unanimously adopted, and the meeting adjourned.

LIEUT.-COL. THOMSON, *Chairman.*
ANDREW I. QUINDLEY. *Secretary.*

LINES ON THE DEATH OF MAJOR H. S. McCONNELL.

In thy young manhood thou art slain,
  Shot! dead! it must be so;
Yet I've tried to think it all a dream,
  The dreadful news, the night of woe.

But all in vain, it is no dream,
  Alas! alas! 'tis true
We've looked our last on the lov'd face,
  Have bid a last adieu.

At day and night we miss you so,
  Our bright and gifted one;
Yes, as we miss when night comes on
  The radiance of the sun.

Among the first to volunteer,
  Prompt to his country's call
Was our true and gallant patriot,
  Our brave and noble " Hall."

On Oak Hill's bloody field he fought,
  And in many a fearful fray
He lead his comrades, nor faltered
  However bore the day.

Ask those who fought beside him,
  How did our hero fall.
"Bravely as he had lived he died,
  They answer one and all.

"Go on; go on," were his last words,
  He could not bid them come,
And thus he died for freedom
  And those he loved, his home.

Rest brave soldier, God is good,
  And thou art free from pain,
Our souls shall rest in the sweet thought
  That we shall meet again.

—SALLIE R.

CAMP NEAR LITTE ROCK,
April 7, 1863.

EDITOR TRUE DEMOCRAT—I suggest we should adopt a new character by which to designate our currency. The old dollar-mark now in use is peculiar alone to the currency of our enemy. It was originally the characters U. S. written one across the other, from which the present character has been abreviated or corrupted. I nominate the letters C. S., written one across the other. from which to characterize the currency of the Confederate States. It is much more elegant than the old one. and is national in significance.

Very respectfully,

W. HICKS.

Mrs. JONES. wife of the representative from Hot Spring County. has spun the chain and filling, and woven 771 yards of cloth within the past thirteen months, and since August, 1861, has woven 1.400 yards.

The Letter From Home.

How sweet 'mid the din and confusion of camps,
The duty, the drill, and the cavalier's tramp,
To know that some loved one does fervently pray
For the poor soldier lad, tho' he's far, far away,
And yearns for the time when war's stern decree
Will yield back the treasure blithe, happy and free.
Such scenes in the distance oft cheers the lone heart,
But a letter from home makes all sorrow depart.

The loved thing may be from your father or mother,
From dear sister Jane, or from *Ike*, your young brother,
And it tells you how loved ones are looking with joy
To a time when they'll meet with their brave soldier boy;
And speaks of "Ma's" kindness in hoarding away
Some nice things for you on that bright happy day;
And "Pa" hopes the time very quickly may come—
Thus you're cheered and consoled by a letter from home.

And mayhap the missive the post-boy does bring
Is from *her* of whom the poets and lovers will sing;
The girl who in leaving you fondly caressed,
Your arm round her waist, and her head on your breast;
And neath Heaven's canopy plighted forever
In bonds of sweet love no tyrant can sever;
Whose fair words you cherish wherever you roam,
And they are doubly enhanced by a letter from home.

God bless our loved ones wherever they be
May our country still rank the glorious and free,
Our prayers be for blessings on loved ones afar
Who're toiling for freedom 'mid hardships of war;
And never neglect writing many a letter
To the brave soldier lad for it makes him feel better;
For in all his misfortunes though distant he roam,
He's cheered when he gets the fond letter from home.

—L. II. M.

Huntsville, Ala., April 10, 1863.

A Gem.

Among the numerous poetic effusions inspired by the war, we have not met anything more sweet and touching than the following lines:

The maid who binds her warrior's sash,
  And, smiling, all her pain dissembles,
The while, beneath her drooping lash,
  One starry tear-drop hangs and trembles.
Though heaven alone records the tear,
  And fame shall never know her story,
Her heart has shed a drop as dear
  As ever dewed the field of glory.

The wife who girds her husband's sword,
  'Mid little ones, who weep and wonder,
And bravely speaks the cheering word,
  What, though her heart be rent asunder;
Doomed nightly in her dreams to hear
  The bolts of war around him rattle—
Has shed as sacred blood as e'er
  Was poured upon the plains of battle.

The mother who conceals her grief,
  While to her breast her son she presses,
Then breathes a few brave words and brief,
  Kissing the patriot brow she blesses,
With no one but her secret God
  To know the pain that weighs upon her,
Sheds holy blood as e'er the sod
  Received on freedom's field of honor.

TENNESSEE.

[Written for THE AVALANCHE.]

Farewell, oh Union!—once beloved
    So tenderly by me;
Thy banner's folds shall never more
    Wave over Tennessee.
I go to join my sister States,
    The gallant band of braves,
Whose starry flag shall soar above
    A free land or our graves.

Sisters, I come with heart and hand!
    Hearts that have ne'er known fear;
Hearts that are strong to aid the cause
    To every breast so dear,
With earnest will to do and dare.
    The Southland shall be free!
With eager step we hasten on—
    Make room for Tennessee.

Oh, Union! long I've clung to thee,
    And for thy sake have borne
From the sweet South, so dear to me,
    Words of reproach and scorn;
But now I cast thy flag away—
    Yes, cast it with disdain—
Dishonored by a bigot's rule,
    And abolition's stain.

If envy could find place with me,
    I'd envy South Carolina;
But, nay! with patriot love
    My great heart doth enshrine her;
And thou shalt find, my sister States,
    When we our foes are meeting,
That Tennessean guns and blades
    Will give them bloody greeting.

Our Southland rises in her might,
 Her eagle spirit blazing!
Her hosts, with prayers upon their lips,
 The battle-cry yet raising:
Sons of the South, to Arms! to Arms!
 Proudly our banner waves.
Oh, never let its proud folds droop,
 But o'er thy bloody graves!

      —LENA LYLE.

MARYLAND.

The despot's heel is on thy shore,
  Maryland!
His touch is at thy temple door,
  Maryland!
Avenge the patriotic gore
That flecked the streets of Baltimore,
And be the battle queen of yore,
  Maryland! My Maryland!

Hark to a wandering son's appeal.
  Maryland!
My mother State, to thee I kneel,
  Maryland!
For life and death, for woe and weal,
Thy peerless chivalry reveal
And gird thy beauteous limbs with steel—
  Maryland! My Maryland!

Thou wilt not cower in the dust,
  Maryland!
Thy beaming sword shall never rust,
  Maryland!
Remember Carroll's sacred trust,

Remember Howard's warlike thrust,
And all thy slumberers with the just,
    Maryland!   My Maryland!

Come, 'tis the red dawn of the day,
    Maryland!
Come, with thy panoplied array,
    Maryland!
With Ringold's spirit for the fray,
With Watson's blood at Monterey,
With fearless Lowe and dashing May—
    Maryland!   My Maryland!

Come while thy shield is bright and strong,
    Maryland!
Come from thy daliance over the wrong,
    Maryland!
Come to thine own heroic throng,
That stalks with liberty along,
And give a new key to the song—
    Maryland!   My Maryland!

Dear mother, burst thy tyrant chain,
    Maryland!
Virginia should not call in vain,
    Maryland!
She meets her sisters on the plain—
"*Sic semper*"—'tis the sweet refrain
That baffles minions back amain.
Arise in majesty again,
    Maryland!   My Maryland!

I see the blush upon thy cheek,
    Maryland!
For thou wert ever bravely meek,
    Maryland!
But hark! there surges forth a shriek
From hill to hill, from creek to creek,

Potomac calls to Chesapeake,
　　Maryland!　My Maryland!

Thou wilt not yield the vandal toll,
　　Maryland!
Thou wilt not crook to his control,
　　Maryland!
Better the fire upon thee roll,

Better the blade, the shot, the bowl
Than crucifixion of the soul,
　　Maryland!　My Maryland!

HUMOR OF THE MARCH.

In the spring of 1863, at Cockran's Cross-Roads, in North Mississippi, we engaged in a lively skirmish with Grierson's Federal cavalry. At first they gave way before us in a very satisfactory manner, but being reinforced, they sent our boys back on the reserve after the latest improved double quick style. A read-headed corporal named Tom Murphy dashed by me, and as he halted, exclaimed, " Well, Captain, we made one of 'em holler!" " What did he say, Tom?" the Captain inquired. Tom looked up, squinted his gray eyes, and replied, " He said, 'Forward, skirmishers!'"

Farewell to Johnson's Island.

Hoarse sounding billows of the white-capped lake
That 'gainst the barriers of our hated prison break.
Farewell! farewell! thy giant inland sea;
Thou, too, subservest the modes of tyranny—
Girding this isle, washing its lonely shore
With moaning echoes of thy melancholy roar.
Farewell thou lake! farewell thou inhospitable land!
Thou hast the curses of this patriot band—
All, save the spot, the holy sacred bed,
Where rest in peace our Southern warriors dead.

[Penciled by an unknown hand upon the prison wall of Johnson Island building.]

On the peninsula the gallant and jolly General J. Bankhead Magruder had ordered a meal for himself and staff. A hungry Reb., and who ever saw one that was not hungry, came up to the farm house, espied the nicely filled table, and without leave or license, sat down and began to annihilate things. Just then the General and friends walked in, escorted by the host. All were surprised. "Hallo! said the fiery Magruder, in terms more explicit than polite: do you know whose table that is you are eating at?" "No, sir;" said John Reb. with his mouth full; "Who is it?" "General Magruder's, sir;"

the commander of this department." "All right.
General," with another big mouthful, "these was
times I ain't particular where I eat, or who I
eat with: sit down and make yourself at home."
The foraging private was unceremoniously
fired out, but not before he had nearly gotten
outside of a pretty square meal.

—

MANASSAS.

[First battle of Bull Run, July 21, 1861.]

BY CATHERINE M. WARFIELD.

They have have met at last—as storm clouds
    Meet in Heaven;
And their thunders have been stilled,
And their leaders crushed or killed,
And their ranks were terror-thrilled,
    Rent and riven.

Like the leaves of Vallombrosa
    They are lying
In the moonlight—in the nidnight,
    Dead and dying.
Like those leaves before the gale
Swept their legions wild and pale,
While the host that made them quail
    Stood defying.

When aloft in morning sunlight
       Flags were flaunted,
And swift vengeance on the Rebel
       Proudly vaunted,
Little did they think that night
Should close upon their shameful flight,
And Rebels victors in the flight
       Stand undaunted.

But peace to those who perished
       In our passes;
Light be the earth above them,
       Green the grasses!
Long shall Northmen rue the day
When they met our stern array,
And shrunk from battle's wild affray
       At Manassas!

A Confederate Wedding.

Come, boys! we've had enough of camp
  And famous battle ground,
So when we trim the waning lamp
  And pass the wine around,
I'll tell a tale of soldier life
  More fit for peaceful time,
Of how I won the sweetest wife
  Within the Southern chime.

    *   *   *   *   *   *

I rode one beautiful morn in spring
  Along 'mid the lonely pines,
And saw not a trace of living thing,
  Nor of homestead roof the signs,
'Till a turn revealed a cottage neat

Where the spinning wheel was heard,
And a maiden song with voice so sweet
　　That it shamed the mocking bird.

Then gazing long to myself I said—
　　By those bonnie eyes of blue,
This heart-fair maiden shall remain unwed
　　Or find its mate in you.
Thus, resolved, I returned next day
　　With my chosen comrades three;
Then asked a drink, and was pressed to stay
　　With a welcome kind and free.

We lingered long, and I came again—
　　A soldier must quickly woo,
So ere recalled to the battle plain
　　Of my love the household knew;
Then the mother sighed, and father said:
　　"My daughter can this be true?"
That you with a stranger youth must wed
　　Unknown scarce a month ago.

Her blue eyes shone with a tear unshed
　　Like a violet wet with dew,
But she turned to me and softly said:
　　"I'm yours—I go with you."
So finding her mind was firmly set
　　They bade me in peace abide;
But first from the town a license get
　　And priest from the country's side.

The preacher he was tall and green
　　As ever did circuit ride—
Had many a rustic wedding seen,
　　But never a couple tied;
Still he did his priestly part right well
　　With but two or three mistakes,
Perhaps he was aided by the smell
　　Of hot pies and corn-meal cakes.

The bride was fairest among the fair,
  Yet not for her bridal array;
She wore but a white rose in her hair,
  And her dress was homespun gray.
When our simple feast at last was o'er
  Instead of a merry dance,
Our boys must show how themselves they bore
  In making the first advance.

The Colonel was so gallant and true
  As he was a soldier brave,
And when of my wedding bliss he knew
  Soon a leave of absence gave;
But many long miles we had to roam,
  Took many a weary ride,
But safe to my distant city home
  I carried my woodland bride.

* * * * * *

Now, boys, my story is told at last,
  The lamp again burns dim,
But let the wine once more be past
  And fill up to the brim—
And may this toast an echo find
  From every heart and mouth,
And here's a health to womankind
  And to our own dear South.

PINELAND, June 8, 1870.

GOOBER PEAS.

BY A. PENDER.

[One of the most widely known Confederate songs. The melody, suited a soldier in his gayest mood, he rolled out: "Peas! peas! peas!" with a gusto that was charming.]

Sitting by the roadside on a summer day,
Chatting with my messmates, passing time away;
Lying in the shadow underneath the trees,
Goodness! how delicious, eating goober peas!

    CHORUS—Peas! peas! peas! peas! eating goober peas!
          Goodness! how delicious, eating goober peas.

When a horseman passes the soldiers have a rule
To cry out at their loudest: "Mister, here's your mule."
But another pleasure enchantinger than these
Is wearing out your grinders eating goober peas.

    CHORUS—

Just before the battle the general hears a row.
He says: "The Yanks are coming. I hear the rifles now."
He turns around in wonder, and what do you think he sees?
The Georgia militia eating goober peas.

    CHORUS—

I think my song has lasted almost long enough.
The subject is interesting, but the rhymes are mighty
    tough.
I wish this war was over, when, free from rags and fleas,
We'd kiss our wives and sweethearts and gobble goober
    peas!

    CHORUS—

Capture of Harper's Ferry.

Crossing with the army into Maryland, A. P. Hill performed a most important part in the capture of Harper's Ferry. Hill's forced march from Harper's Ferry to Sharpsburg and his rush into the battle at the critical juncture, changing the whole face of affairs and converting threatened disaster into splendid victory, are among the most brilliant achievements of the war. December 13 he contributed his share to winning a victory near "Hamilton's Crossing." With Jackson on his march to Chancellorsville, and flank march to Hooker's rear, he was moving his division into line of battle to take the advance, when Jackson was shot down by his own men, and, after giving his chief needed personal attention, Hill hurried to assume command and finish the brilliant movement which Jackson had so auspiciously begun, but he was soon after wounded himself and compelled to relinquish the command and leave to "Jeb" Stuart, the dashing, glorious "Jeb" Stuart, who was sent for and put in command, the glory of carrying line after line of the enemy's breastworks, as he gave the old corps the watchword, "Charge, and remember Jackson," and rode at the head of the charging columns, singing in clear notes heard above the din of battle:

Old Joe Hooker, won't you come out of the wilderness?

Hill was soon after promoted, made lieutenant general, and put in command of the Third corps. His health failed, and he was advised to take a rest at the house of a relative in Chesterfield County, but he had left strict injunctions with his staff to be notified of any movement of the enemy, and on April 2, in making a brave attempt to take personal command of a part of his corps, which had been cut off, he was shot down and instantly killed by a squad of the enemy whose surrender he had demanded. His body was recovered by a charge of the members of his staff. No general orders announced his death, no honor attended his burial, for the grand old army had taken up its sad march to Appomattox Court House. But he lived in the hearts of his old corps of loving comrades; he will live in life-speaking bronze that loving hearts have reared.

The Boy Soldier.

By a Lady of Savannah, Ga.

He is acting o'er the battle,
  With his cap and feather gay;
Singing out his soldier prattle
  In a mockish manly way;

With the boldest, bravest foot-step
  Treading firmly up and down,
And his banner waving softly
  O'er his boyish locks of brown.

And I sit beside him sewing,
  With a busy heart and hand,
For the gallant soldier going
  To the far-off battle-land.
And I gaze upon my jewel,
  In his baby-spirit bold—
My little, blue-eyed soldier,
  Just a second summer old.

I would speed him to the battle,
  I would arm him for the fight,
I would give him for his country—
  For his country's wrong and right.
I would nerve his hand with blessings
  From the God of Battles won.
With his helmet and his armor,
  I would cover o'er my son.

Oh! I know there'd be a struggle,
  For I love my darling boy.
He's the gladness of my spirit;
  He's the sunlight of my joy.
Yet, in thinking of my country,
  Oh, my spirit groweth bold,
And I wish my blue-eyed soldier
  Were but *twenty* summers old.

PENSACOLA.

BY M. LOUISE ROGERS.

O, night wind! gently, softly blow
Over the loved ones lying so low
  On a soldier's hard rough pillow,
Where camp-fires on the plains are traced,
And the shore is clasped in rude embrace
  By the deep Gulf's rolling billow.

O, night wind! come with your purest breath,
And kiss them asleep, but not in death—
  Kiss them softly and sweetly.
Let no poison lurk in your tender caress;
Let no Upas kill our heart's own best,
  But kiss them purely and gently.

O, night wind! they are dreaming of friends and home,
Then, lightly rest when to them you come.
  Dispell not the love-lit vision
With a rude caress; but let them sleep on,
While we kiss them in dreams one by one,
  And commit them to God and Heaven.

O, do you not know gentle night wind,
Our hearts have gone and entered in
  Those camps by the sea-girt strand?
More than half our lives—do you not know?—
Has flown to the clime where orange buds blow
  Throughout the star-bright land.

My brother! my brother!   O, sweet night wind!
No love-lit eyes to meet him, so kind,
  On Pensacola's plains.
No lips to kiss thy weary brow;
No voice to speak tender and low:
  No hand to charm away thy pain.

No father to kneel with him in prayer;
No mother to watch with tender care;

No sister when morning awakes.
Alone! alone!   But, O, night wind!
Tell him we'll be so hopeful and kind,
    And smile for his sweet sake.

Let Death wave not his gloomy wing
Over the darling hopes we sing.
    Tell him to flee from the track
Where the feet of our loved ones press the sod.
Or march to the tramp of the stern War God.
    Tell him to let them *come back.*

And, oh! night wind! will you not bear
Up to the Throne our tears and prayers,
    That God will guide and shield
The dear loved ones our country has claimed
To bear her hopes and fair, proud name
    On the cruel battlefield?

Oh! weeping heart! be still again!
On Pensacola's sun-burnt plain,
    The God we worship is *there*—
His arm is there as strong to save
From death, the foeman and the grave,
    As *here,* where we kneel in prayer.

LAND OF KING COTTON.

BY JOE AUGUSTINE SIGNAIGO.

(Air, "Red, White and Blue.")
Oh, Dixie, the land of King Cotton,
    The home of the brave and the free;
A nation of freedom begotten,
    The terror of despots to be.
Wherever thy banner is streaming
    Base tyranny quails at thy feet,

And liberty's sunlight is beaming
  In splendor of majesty sweet.

    CHORUS—Three cheers for our army so true,
        Three cheers for Price, Johnson
          and Lee.
        Beauregard and our Davis forever!
        The pride of the brave and the free.

When liberty sounds her war rattle,
  Demanding her rights and her due,
The first land that rallies to battle
  Is Dixie, the shrine of the true.
Thick as leaves of the forest in summer,
  Her brave sons will rise on each plain,
And then strike until each vandal comer
  Lies dead in the soil he would stain.

    CHORUS—

May the names of the dead that we cherish
  Fill memory's cup to the brim;
May the laurels they've won never perish,
  Nor "star of their glory grow dim."
May the States of the South never sever,
  But champions of freedom e'er be.
May they flourish Confederate forever,
  The boast of the brave and the free.

    CHORUS—

GENERAL A. P. HILL.

BY D. J. WILLIAM JONES.

DR. JONES quotes from President Davis in calling him the "gallant and glorious little Powell Hill." A. P. Hill was one of the most thoroughly accomplished soldiers whom the war produced. He was appointed colonel of the Thirteenth Virginia regiment at Harper's Ferry in the early spring of 1861. In the early days of 1862 General Hill received his well-deserved promotion, and, with his commission, a brigadier general, was put in command of the famous old brigade which Longstreet had commanded. I never shall forget the thrilling scene in Jackson's corps as A. P. Hill's guns opened at Mechanicsville that memorable afternoon of the 26th of June, 1862, and the "foot cavalry" made the hills and valleys ring with their Confederate yells as they eagerly pressed forward in anticipation of victory. Hill moved forward in fine style and drove the enemy from their position at Mechanicsville, thus opening a way for Longstreet and D. H. Hill, whose divisions were thrown across the Chicahominy at that point. In the early morning of the 27th of June the Confederate troops on the north side were in motion, and the Federal forces, under gallant Fitz John Porter, awaited them in a position naturally strong, but which had been fortified with all the appliances of engineering skill and ample material. Encountering the enemy in his strong position and heavy entrenchments near Cold Harbor about 2 o'clock p. m., Hill bore the brunt of the fight for about two hours, until Jackson got into position and Longstreet went to his assistance, and then bore his full share in the grand charge which swept the field along the whole line of Cold Harbor and Gains' Mill, capturing fourteen pieces of artillery and many prisoners and driving the enemy in great confusion from every position. I may not give in detail the further movements of those seven days of carnage and Confederate victory which raised the siege of Richmond and drove McClellan's splendid army to the cover of his gunboats at Harrison's Landing. He especially distinguished himself and covered with glory his "Light Division" in the battle of Frazier's Farm. It was during this movement President Davis was reconnoitering in front when he met General Lee on the same business and remonstrated with him, saying: "This is no place for the commander of the army." The general rejoined: "It seems to me this is no place for the commander-in-chief of all our armies." Just then "gallant little A. P. Hill" galloped up and exclaimed: "This is no place for either of you, and as commander of this part of the field I order you both to the rear." They moved a little to the rear and became absorbed in a consultation, when Hill galloped up and exclaimed: "Did I not order you away from here, and did you not promise to obey me? Why, one shot from that battery over there might deprive the army of Northern Virginia of its commander and the Confederacy of its President." Afterward he was assigned to Jackson's corps and sent to join him near Gordonville. He was an active participant in the battle of Cedar Run, where Jackson defeated his old "Quartermaster General Banks." I saw him in the crisis, with coat off and sabre drawn, throwing out skirmishers to stop stragglers, tearing off the bars of a lieutenant who was skulking to the rear, and giving his clear, crisp orders as he hurried his veterans into the fight and hurled back the blue lines who were advancing, flushed with victory—he seemed to me the very personification of the genius of battle, the very beau ideal of the soldier. At second Manassas, during the crisis of the struggle for the famous railroad cut, Hill sent a staff officer to inquire of brave old Maxey Gregg how he was getting on. "Tell him," said the old hero, "that our ammunition is exhausted, but rocks are very plentiul, and we will hold our position with them until we can get ammunition." Sending his staff and couriers to fill their haversacks and pockets with cartridges and distribute them to the men, Hill himself galloped to the line and excited the wildest enthusiasm as his clarion voice rang out: "Good for you, boys! Give them the rocks and the

bayonet. and hold your position. I will soon
have ammunition and reinforcements for you."

The Gallant Charge of Cheatham's Division at Franklin, Tenn.

By Col. Robert Gates.

THE battle of Franklin was fought November
30. 1864. The Federals, under General Scho-
field. occupied a strong natural position, which
they made stronger by first-class earthworks.
The approaches were through open fields. from
a mile to a mile and a half in width. In front of
the position assaulted by Cheatham's old division.
groves of locust trees had been cut down, behind
which the first line of Federals received the
assault. General Cheatham was commanding
the corps and General John C. Brown the old
division. The division moved to the assault
with the left on the Columbia pike. Moving
parallel, with its right on the Franklin pike, was
Cleburne's division. There had long been a
generous rivalry between those two commands.
Owing to its splendid achievements at Ringgold.
Cleburne's division "held the edge" on the
famous Tennesseeans. Hence again at Franklin, as on the 22d of July, before Atlanta, these

two divisions raced for first honors. In splendid style, their officers gallantly urging them on, the crack divisions of the western army moved through shot and shell to the desperate work before them. It was a splendid sight. The entire field was in full view, over which the eighteen brigades of Hood's army moved to the assault. From the rifle pits and the locust zeralas in front of the main works of the Federal infantry, poured a terrific fire, while from the main works and the heights beyond the river more than a hundred cannon volleyed and thundered on the advancing host.

THE CHARGE OVER THE PLAIN.

But there was no halting or wavering, and over the fire-swept plain the column advanced, closing up the dreadful gaps of death like the "Old Guard" at Waterloo. With a yell and a rush at the point of the bayonet, the first line of works was carried. On and on, with guns at right-shoulder-shift, dashed the heroic lines. Yet a half mile of open ground remains to be crossed. The firing from the main works was now terrific. Not a soldier of that gallant army had ever experienced a fire so dreadful. The hundred cannon, double-shotted, swept the plain, and the roll of 20,000 muskets was incessant and appalling. But on swept the Confederates, never firing a gun, never cheered by the boom of a cannon of their own, never wavering, eyes to the front, "victory or death" ringing in every heart, officers and men fell like dead leaves when forests are shaken. The glorious Cleburne fell, and the dashing Granbury, of Cheatham's old division. Strahl, Carter and Gist fell, and Brown and Gordon were wounded; and yet on swept the glorious line of gray. At last the plain behind them, strewn with the dead and wounded, outnumbering the living, the assaulting column reeled against the strong works behind which the Federal army fought in comparative security, and, with the nerve and cool destructiveness that became veterans. The works reached, a ditch must be crossed and an embankment climbed. The Federal fire became now more terrific, all their reserves being brought into action. Then it was that on the right and left the Confederates recoiled and reeled back against the fatal plain to the rifle pits and locust zerales just taken. Of all that assaulting column, Cheatham's old division alone held its ground. This division, with every general and field officer, except Colonel Hurt, who commanded the Sixth and Ninth, with half its number strewn on the plains, scrambled across the ditch and climbed upon the works, driving the Federals out and taking possession.

Having repulsed the Confederates at all other points, the Federals rallied, and charged Cheatham's devoted division, confident of annihilating or capturing it. The division, quickly noting their peril, placed the embankment of works just taken between them and the Federals, and held their perilous position with matchless heroism and unequaled valor to the end. Assailed in the front, subject to a terrific cross-fire from angles in the works to the right and to the left, the old division stood firm, and poured a destructive fire into their assailants in front. Alone they stood amid ten thousand—volleyed and thundered at from three sides—stood and died and conquered. The Federals gained the opposite side of the earthworks, but could not cross or dislodge their enemy. They glared into each other's eyes and fought with clubbed guns, but like gladiators, toe to toe, fought and died, but never turned back or wavered. It was a sublime moment. The old division was standing on the sacred soil of its grand, old mother, Tennessee. It was making a last heroic effort for home and cause. The eyes of mother, wife and sweetheart, in hearing, as it were, of the battle's thunder, watched and, waiting, wept. Its comrades, after prodigies of valor, had reeled back from the impossible. It stood alone of all the assaulting host, using the enemy's works against himself—alone, in the fiery-red jaws of a hell of battle. The Spartans at Thermopylæ, the Light Brigade at Balaklava, the Old Guards at Waterloo, do not overmatch it in situation or equal it in results. It stood there in the jaws of death—stood and conquered. The night was hideous with the red glare of battle. The dead and wounded encumbered their movements; exhaustion threatened: and, yet, they stood and conquered. It was the old division's last supreme effort while hope yet remained—its last confident struggle for cause and home, and it stood like the Old Ironsides at Nasby—stood and sublimely conquered. Early after the darkness set in, the Confederates rallied and renewed the assault on the right and left. The enemy gave way, and Franklin was taken. But when the Confederates poured in there, amidst the dying, their visages blackened with smoke beyond recognition, stood Cheatham's division, masters of the works they had taken at the first—master of the field—the unquestioned heroes of the battle, the matchless division of the Western Army. There it stood, amid the wrecks of battle; amid its dead, that outnumbered the living; without a general officer left; with but one field officer able for duty; the division commanded by colonels, regiments by captains and lieutenants, and companies by sergeants and corporals. The charge of Cheatham's division stands out as one of the grand acts of cool courage and superb daring in the martial history of the world, and in future years it will be pointed out by historians as one of the grandest of all great military achievements in war.

Among the gallant soldiers of Cheatham's division still living, none were braver or are more worthy of mention than Dr. Sam Wilkerson, of Morrilton, Ark. While in the front of the battle he was wounded—lost a leg in his country's cause—still lives, and glories to-day in the grand achievements of Cheatham's band.

THE BATTLE AT FRANKLIN.

A SCHOOL girl of 1864 writes: "I was a pupil in the old Franklin Female Institute. While we were trying to concentrate our minds on our books, one ear was always open to the sounds of fife and rattle of drums, the clatter of horses' hoofs and the electrifying notes of the bugle. We were always allowed to run to the front gate to see the soldiers pass. If they were "our boys" we waived bonnets, and handerchiefs if they were Yankees, and we watched Buell's army of thousands pass, we looked and felt dismayed.

"On an ever memorable day, the 30th of November, we assembled at school as usual. Our teachers' faces looked unusually serious that morning. The Federal couriers were dashing hither and thither. The officers were gathering in squads, and the cavalry, with swords and sabres clanking, were driving their spurs into their horses' flanks and galloping out to first one picket post and then another, on the roads leading south and southwest of town. The bell called us in the chapel. We were to take our books and go home, as there was every indication that we would be in the midst of a battle that day.

At 4 o'clock that afternoon I stood in our front door and heard musketry in the neighborhood of Colonel Carter's, on the Columbia pike. To this day I can recall the feeling of sickening dread that came over me. As the evening wore on the firing became more frequent, and nearer and louder; then the cannon began to roar from the fort. My father, realizing that we were in range of guns from both armies, told us to run down into the cellar. We hastily threw a change of clothing into a bundle and obeyed at once. My mother, who never knew what fear meant

in her life, was a little reluctant to go and leave
the upper part of the house to the tender mer-
cies of soldiers, but she finally joined us in the
basement. A few minutes later there was a
crash, and down came a deluge of dust and
gravel. The usually placid face of our old
black mammy, now thoroughly frightened, appeared on the scene. She said a cannon ball
had torn a hole in the side of the meat house
and broken her wash kettle to pieces. She left
the supper on the stove and fled precipitately
into the cellar. After that the only way we
could get anything to eat was by sending a guard,
who was in the yard, to the kitchen after it.
The patter of the bullets on the blinds was anything but soothing. The incessant booming of
cannon and the rattle of the guns continued
until midnight; then the firing gradually
ceased. We, of course, were in ignorance of
who was in possession of the place, but
all the while hoping and praying that it
might be our boys. About one o'clock
we thought the town was being reduced to
ashes, but it turned out to be the Odd Fellows
Hall on the square. About four o'clock we
heard the tramping of feet and the sound of
voices. Our hearts jumped into our mouths,
and what joy when we learned that our own
soldiers were in possession of the town! We

first learned it from the men who carried Col. Sam Shannon, who had been wounded, to his sister's house—our next door neighbor. Our men were in pessession of the town. We did not stand on ceremony getting out of that cellar. Our doors were thrown wide open, and in a few moments a big fire was burning in the parlor.

The first man to enter was Gen. Wm. Bate, all bespattered with mud and blackened with powder, but a grand and glorious soldier under it all. I will not attempt to picture the meeting between him and my father who had been life long friends. Next came Gen. Tom Benton Smith with the impersonation of a chivalric, gallant soldier, wearing under the mud and dirt his recent hard earned honors. Poor fellow, how short-lived were his joys! A cruel sabre cut at Nashville forever dethroned his reason. Space fails me to mention the list who came that day and received a warm welcome. I shall mention a reproof my sisters received from some of their soldier sweethearts. An uncle of ours, who made his home in New York city, had my sisters visit him, and of course, they replenished their wardrobes while there. On the morning after the battle they wanted to compliment their soldier friends by "looking their best," so they put on their prettiest dresses. The soldiers

were so unaccustomed to seeing stylish new
dresses, that they doubted their loyalty, thought
they should have on homespun dresses instead
of "store clothes," In the afternoon, December 1st, some of us went to the battle-field to
give water and wine to the wounded. All of us
carried cups from which to refresh the thirsty.
Horrors! What sights that met our girlish
eyes! The dead and wounded lined the Columbia pike for the distance of a mile. In Mrs.
Sykes' yard Gen. Hood sat talking with some
of his staff officers. I didn't look upon him as
a hero, because nothing had been accomplished
that could benefit us. As we approached Col.
Carter's house, we could scarcely walk without
stepping on dead or dying men. We could
hear the cries of the wounded, of which Col.
Carter's house was full to overflowing. As I
entered the front door I heard a poor fellow
giving his sympathetic comrades a dying message for his loved ones at home. We went
through the hall and were shown into a little
room where a soft light revealed all that was
mortal of the gifted young genius, Theo. Carter,
who, under the pseudonym of "Mint Julep,"
wrote such delightful letters to the *Chattanooga
Rebel.* Bending over him, begging for just one
word of recognition, was his faithful and heart-
broken sister. The night before the battle he

had taken supper at Mr. Green Neely's (the father of our postmaster), and was in perfect ecstacy of joy at the thought of seeing his family on the morrow, from whom he had been saparated so long. But alas! when the morrow came, that active, brilliant brain had been pierced by one of the enemy's bullets; he was carried home and ministered to by those faithful sisters, and died, I think, without ever having spoken a word. From this sad scene we passed on to a locust thicket, and men in every conceivable position could be seen, some with their fingers on the triggers and death struck them so suddenly they did not move. Past the thicket we saw trenches dug to receive as many as ten bodies. On the left of the pike, around the old gin house, men and horses were lying so thick we could not walk. Gen. Adams' horse was lying stark and stiff upon the breastworks. Ambulances were being filled with the wounded as fast as possible, and the whole town was turned into an hospital. Our house was as full as could be; from morning until night we made bandages and scraped linen lint with which to dress their wounds, besides making jellies and soups with which to nourish them. The times were not without their romances. Only a short time afterward a handsome young Missouri surgeon in charge of one of the hospitals married one of our most prominent young ladies. Another who was wounded here married also.

Humor of the March.

When a company of home guards on the Mississippi river had fired upon a gun boat the boat acknowledged by opening on them with shell. The guards immediately got down close to the ground, and one of them said, "Boys, if I ain't flat enough won't one of you please get on me and mash me flatter?"

The Dying Soldier.

By Sallie Ada Reedy.

My noble Commander, thank God you have come;
You know the dear ones who are waiting at home,
And oh, it was dreadful to die here alone,
No hand on my brow, my comrades all gone.

I thought I would die many hours ago,
And those who are waiting me never could know
That here with the faith of its happier years,
My soul has not wandered one moment from theirs.

The dead are around but my soul was away
'Mid the roses that blossom 'round my cottage to-day;
I thought that I sat where the jassamines twine
And gathered the delicate buds from the vine.

And there like a bird that has folded its wings,
At home 'mid the smile of all beautiful things,
With sweet words of welcome and kisses of love,
Was one I will miss in yon heaven above.

By the light that I saw on her radiant brow
She watches and waits there, and prays for me now—
My Captain bend low for this poor wounded side
Is draining my heart of its last crimson tide.

Some day when you leave this dark place and go free,
You'll meet a fair girl; she will question of me;
She has kissed this bright curl as it lay on my head,
When it goes back alone she will know I am dead;
And tell her the soul, which on earth was her own,
Is waiting and weeping in heaven alone.

My mother, God help her, her grief will be wild
When she hears the mad ,Hessians have murdered her
        child;
But tell her ('twill be one sweet chime in my knell)
That the flag of my country now waves where I fell.

It is well—it is well thus to die in my youth,
A martyr to freedom and justice and truth;
Farewell to earth's hopes, precious dreams of my heart,
My life's going out but my love shall not depart,
And now, on the wings my soul has unfurled,
Going up, soft and sweet, to yon beautiful world.

How beautiful in death,
  The warrior' corse appears,
Embalmed by fond affection's breath
  And bath'd in woman's tears.

—MONTGOMERY.

There were sad hearts in a darkened home,
  When the brave had left their bower,
But the strength of prayer and sacrifice
  Was with them in that hour.

—MRS. HEMANS.

An Address to the Confederate Soldiers of the Southwest.

By S. H. Ford, LL.D.

Grenada, Miss., October, 1862.

Today, if you hear His voice, harden not your heart.—Paul.

Soldiers and Brothers—One who has passed with you through many a sad and many a glorious scene; who has sat with you around your camp fires when the freezing wind swept by; has slept in your tents when the straw froze to the ground; has joined in your foot-sore marches; stood near you in the day of battle; visited you in the hospitals; followed your comrades to the grave, and communicated the last death whispers of love to far-off friends—one who, though never connected with the service, has never ceased since this war began to labor and to pray for you—addreses these pages to you, desirous thereby to direct your minds to the lessons to be gathered from the fields where you have nobly battled and suffered.

History is God's voice, speaking to us from the past, of peoples and empires, of battles and sieges, victories and defeats. But if that voice, pealing down through the silent centuries, has power to awaken, to inspire and to teach, what should be its influence when it speaks direct from scenes and events which we have witnessed, and where we ourselves have been actors? Your deeds, your endurances, has rendered many an obscure spot immortal. Bowling Green and Columbus are now historic ground. The fields of Elkhorn, Belmont and Shiloh will live in story and in song. Vicksburg and Baton Rouge, Lexington, Mo., and Richmond, Ky., have been made sacred by your valor. You have wrought out a history of the Southwest fit to live beside that written in glorious deeds by your brothers of the Southeast. We had neither arms nor munitions of war, and our ports were sealed, yet we have armed a vast army which has won victory on a hundred fields. The poor, unenterprising, enervated South, without provisions or manufactories—without clothing or medicines—a proud foe, with all the facilities to equip an overwhelming army. God has brought strength out of weakness; under His blessing we have made our enemies respect our power. Our disasters were enough to shake the stoutest hearts. When, after hopeful accounts from the siege of Fort Donelson, the news at last came that it had fallen; that 12,000 heroes who had driven triple their number day after day before them, at length overcome by fatigue, hunger and cold, had to surrender; that, as a consequence, Nashville, with all its stores, and all Middle Tennessee, were abandoned to the foe. How dark the day seemed! Like the rush of Alpine torrents came the tidings, freezing our very blood and overwhelming us with sorrow. Still, onward rolled the dark, rushing tide of invasion. In the last Norfolk was abandoned and Williamsburg and Yorktown were evacuated. Richmond was besieged and New Orleans taken. Fort Pillow was abandoned and Memphis and Helena were occupied by the foe. But these stunning blows struck from the hearts of the people a fire which swept through the South wrapping it in the flames of patriotism. When Donelson fell there were not more than 240,000 men in all our armies, and enlistments had almost ceased. There was not ammunition enough in the whole Confederacy to continue the battle all around the lines three days. But the fall of Donelson was as the voice of God, waking new energies and calling every man into action. Our armies soon swelled to double their numbers. Arms sufficient, through the same watchful Providence, were obtained. Our disasters proved to be blessings in disguise. But if from the bitterness of disaster sweets have been extracted, what language shall record the gracious providences of God in the astonishing victories with which He has crowned our arms? Seventy-five thousand and then forty thousand additional men were called out in the commencement of the war to crush and subjuagte the starving, "the unarmed South." Under the supervision of the greatest General of the age, "Winfield Scott," the grand army moved "on to Richmond," 50,000 men. The mighty host was met at Manassas by an inferior force. The Southern Republic trembled for the fate of that eventful day and of their comparitively small army. The battle raged—at times it seemed to quiver in the balance. But the *result!* Broken, scattered. flying. routed. defeated—"the grand army.'

From Bethel and Vienna, from Bull Run and Ball's Bluff, from the battle scenes of Virginia of '61 and '62 God's voice speaks in thrilllng eloquence.

Nor can we forget the glorious feats in Missouri—Springfield, Lexington, Oak Hills, Elkhorn, nor the brilliant achievements at Shiloh. From the clouds that lowered through a weary winter and spring, again streamed the smile of God; and like bust of splendor from the opening heaven came the victories of the glorious summer.

And what shall be said of the scenes on the Rapidan and the Rappahannock, of Manassas. of Harper's Ferry and Hagerstown Heights. The curtain is now trembling on the wheel of time, when it is lifted a glorious peace may have been conquered.

Can any man look at all these victories—over armies the best appointed the world ever beheld. by barefooted half clad suffering Southerners and not gratefully acknowledge that Jehovah has been with us?

One of the bloodiest battles of the Civil War was fought at Chickamauga, Ga., September 19-20, 1863, between Rosecrans (Federal), who commanded 55,000 men, and Bragg (Confederate), whose army numbered 70,00. The Federals were defeated, losing 16,000 men. The Confederates lost 18,000. Bragg was slowly retreating, and expecting reinforcements before he should decide to give battle to Rosecrans. who was marching on to Chattanooga. These reinforcements coming suddenly, Bragg halted at Chickamauga and deployed for battle. Rosecrans placed his force with Thomas on the left. Crittenden in the center and McCook on the right, along Chickamauga creek.

The Confederates crossed the creek September 19, and Thomas' line was struck by Polk. Thomas confused Bragg's plan by speedily returning the assault. Thomas was again attacked September 20, and although he often called for reinforcements he held his position well. Fi-

nally Gen. Wood, through misinterpreting an
order, made a false move, which precipitated
the Confederates upon a weak point in the
Federal line and the day was lost.

Rosecrans fled to Chattanooga. Thomas kept
fighting until Garfield was sent to call him off.
It was here that Thomas acquired the sobriquet
of "The Rock of Chickamauga." Mr. Maurice
Thompson, who was born in Indiana, was edu-
cated on his father's estate in Georgia, and
after the war settled at Crawfordsville, Indiana,
contributes to *The Century* the following ballad
on the battle. Mr. Thompson fought on the
Confederate side.

THE BALLAD OF CHICKAMAUGA.

By Chickamauga's crooked stream the martial trumpets
  blew,
The North and South stood face to face with War's dread
  work to do;
O, lion strong, unselfish, brave, twin athletes battle-wise,
Brothers, yet enemies, the fire of conflict in their eyes.
All banner-led and bugle-stirred, they set them to the
  fight,
Hearing the god of slaughter laugh from mountain height
  to height.

The ruddy, fair-haired, giant North, breathed loud and
  strove amain,
The swarthy soldiers of the South did heave them to the
  strain;
An earthquake shuddered under foot, a cloud rolled over
  head,

And serpent tongues of flames cut through and lapped
    and twinkled red,
Where back and forth a bullet stream went singing like a
    breeze,
What time the snarling cannon balls to splinters tore the
    trees.

"Make way, make way," a voice boomed out, "I'm
    marching to the sea,"
The answer was a Rebel yell and Bragg's artillery.
Where Negley struck, the cohorts gray like storm-tossed
    clouds were rent,
Where Buckner charged a cyclone fell, the blue to tatters
    went;
The noble Brannan cheered his men, Pat Cleburne an-
    swered back,
And Little stormed, and life was naught in Walthall's
    bloody track.

Old Taylor,s Ridge rocked to its base, and Pigeon Moun-
    tain shook,
And Helm went down, and Little died and broken was
    McCook.
Van Cleve moved like a hurricane, a tempest blew with
    Hood,
Awful the sweep of Breckinridge across · the flaming
    wood.
Never before did battle-roar such chords of thunder
    make,
Never again shall tides of men over such barriers break.

"Stand fast, stand fast," cried Rosecrans, and Thomas
    said, " I will,"
And crash on crash his batteries dashed their broadsides
    down the hill.
Brave Longstreet's splendid rush tore through whatever
    barred its track,

I.—9

'Till the Rock of Chickamauga hurled the roaring columns
    back,
And gave the tide of victory the red tinge of defeat,
Adding a noble dignity to that hard word, *retreat.*

Two days they fought, and ever more those days shall
    stand apart,
Keynotes of epic chivalry within the Nation's heart.
Come, come, and set the carven rocks to mark this glorious
    spot,
Here let the deeds of heroes live, their hatreds to forget.
Build, build, but never monument of stone shall last as
    long
As one old soldier's ballad borne on breath of battle song.

General Grant and Jefferson Davis Second Cousins.

It will be news to many persons. even to such
as are pretty well read in the genealogies of
great men, to hear that U. S. Grant and Jefferson Davis were relatives having a common
ancestor in the third generation back, in William
Simpson, of Bucks county, Pa., who was grand-
father to both General Grant's mother and
Jefferson Davis' father.

The "Life of John Davis," we are told is the
logbook by which every real Pennsylvania
Davis swears.

John Davis married Ann Simpson, the

daughter of William Simpson on [June 26,
1783. William Simpson was a soldier of the
revolution. Settled in Bucks county, Pa.,
(Buckingham). He made application to purchase one hundred acres of land January 15,
1766, and the deed was executed by John Penn,
May 23, 1767. He married Nancy Hines of
New Britian, was the father of two sons and two
daughters, John and Mathew, Ann and Marie.
Mathew removed to near Zanesville, Ohio, in
1810; John lived and died in the country. Ann
married John Davis. William Simpson died in
1816, aged eighty-four. General Grant's mother
descended from the Bucks county Simpsons.

Through John Davis, it appears William
Simpson was great-grandfather to Jefferson
Davis as well as Ulysses Simpson Grant thus
making these men direct second cousins. There
are more than five hundred descendants in the
United States at the present time, who are about
equally related to both General Grant and Jefferson Davis.

News Item April 15, 1863.

The situation—On the 19th and 20th of March
snow fell depth of ten inches at Richmond. It
is settled opinion at Richmond that Hooker will
advance when the roads admit of it.

My Southern Home.

To my far away home where the laurel tree blooms,
  My heart ever turns with a sigh;
'Tis the land of my birth where my ancestors' tombs
  Point up to the clear Southern sky.
'Tis the land of the rose, of the myrtle and vine,
  Its carpet the moss covered sod;
'Tis the land which with pride I may ever call mine,
  A land richly blessed by our God.

'Tis the land of the sun where the feathery hosts
  Sing sweet in their Creator's praise,
'Tis the land from whose glens rise the tangible ghosts,
  The memories left of past days.
'Tis the home of the pure and the land of the brave,
  The faithful the true and the just,
'Tis the land on whose breast I would make me my grave
  To rest my inanimate dust.

'Tis the land of the hero, the theme of the bard,
  'Tho true that her flag has furled;
Yet the deeds of her sons and her face battle scarred
  Have challenged the praise of the world.
'Tis the land which hath reared in the temple of fame,
  The loftiest pile that we see,
And her sons ever thrill at the sound of that name,
  Immortal, invincible Lee.

There a father doth rest where the soft breezes play,
  The willows droop over his tomb;
There a mother still grieves for a son far away,
  'Mid winter and withering gloom.
Take me back, let me fly to to the land of my birth,
  To rest—never more will I roam;
Let me hold ever more to the dearest on earth,
  My mother, my country, my home.

A. S. Morton.

St. Paul, Minn., January 20, 1895.

The Flag of the Florida Battery.

Col. W. T. Stockton of the Florida Brigade wrote a poem about this flag. It was used by the Marion Light Artillery in the Battle of Richmond, Kentucky. It was made of a crimson shawl presented by Mrs. J. J. Dickison. The rings attached to the lance made of jewelry contributed by ladies of Marion county, Fla., the ferrule, a silver comb worn by Mrs. Dickison on her bridal day.

Joe Johnston.

Fill the breach for the land of the West!
Thus we give of our bravest and best,
  Of his state and his army the pride—
Hope shines like the plume of Navarre on his crest
  And gleams in the glaive at his side.

For his courage is keen and his honor is bright
As the trusty Toledo* he wears to the fight,
  Newly wrought in the forges of Spain,
And his weapon, like all he has brandished for right,
  Will never be dimmed by a stain.

He leaves the loved soil of Virginia behind,
Where the dust of his father is fitly enshrined,
  Where lies the fresh fields of his fame;
Where the murmuring pines, as they swayed in the
     wind,
  Seem ever to whisper his name.

The Johnstons have always borne wings on their spurs
And their motto a noble distinction confers—
  " Ever ready " for friend or for foe—
With a patriot's fervor the sentiment stirs
  The large, manly heart of our Joe.

We read that a former bold chief of the clan
Fell, bravely defending the West in the van
  On Shiloh's illustrious day,
And with reason we reckon our Johnston the man
  The dark, bloody debt to repay.

There is work to be done; if not glory to seek,
There's a just and a terrible vengence to wreak
  For crime of a terrible dye,
While the plaint of the helpless, the wail of the weak,
  In chorus rise up to the sky.

Brave-born Tennesseeans, so loyal, so true,
Who have hunted the beasts in your highlands—of you
  Our leader had never a doubt;
You will troop by the thousands the chase to renew
  The day that his bugles ring out.

Then once more to the breach for the land of the West,
Strike home for your hearths, for the lips you love best—
  Follow on where your leader you see;
One flash of his sword, when the foe is hard pressed,
  And the land of the West shall be free!

                        —JOHN R. THOMPSON.
Richmond, Va., December 1, 1862.

----

*Gen. Johnston carries a beautiful blade, recently pre-
sented to him, bearing the mark of the Royal Manufactory
of Toledo, 1862.

Burial of the Dead.

By Col. Theo. O'Hara, of Kentucky.

The muffled drum's sad roll has beat
  The soldier's last tattoo;
No more on life's parade shall meet
  The brave and daring few.
On fame's eternal camping ground
  Their silent tents are spread,
And Glory guards and solemn 'round
  The bivouac of the dead.

No answer to the foe's advance
  Now swells upon the wind;
No troubled thought at midnight haunts
  Of loved ones left behind;
No vision of the morrow's strife
  The warrior's dream alarms—
No braying horn nor screaming fife
  At dawn shall call to arms.

Their shivered swords are red with rust,
  Their plumed heads are bowed;
Their haughty banner, trailed in dust,
  Is now their martial shroud.
And plenteous funeral tears have washed
  The red stains from each brow,
And their proud forms, in battle gashed,
  Are freed from anguish now.

The neighing steed, the flashing blade,
  The trumpet's stirring blast;
The charge, the dreadful cannonade,
  The din and shout are past;
No war's wild note, nor glory's peal,
  Shall, with fierce delight,
Those breasts that nevermore shall feel
  The rapture of the fight.

Like the dread Northern hurricane
  That sweeps his broad plateau,
Flushed with the triumph yet to gain,
  Came down the serried foe,
Our heroes felt the shock and leapt
  To meet them on the plain;
And long the pitying sky hath wept
  Above our gallant slain.

Sons of our consecrated ground,
  Ye must not slumber there,
Where strangers' steps and tongues resound
  Along the heedless air;
Your own proud land's heroic soil,
  Shall be your fitter grave—
She claims from war his richest spoil,
  The ashes of her brave.

So 'neath their parent turf they rest,
  Far from the gory field;
Borne to a Spartan mother's breast
  On many a bloody shield.
The sunshine of a native sky smiles sadly on them
    here,
  And kindred hearts and eyes watch by
The hero's sepulcher.

Rest on, embalmed and sainted dead!
  Dear as the bloody brave;
No impious footstep here shall tread
  The herbage of your grave;
Nor shall your glory be forgot
  While fame her record keeps.
On honor points the hallowed spot
  Where valor proudly sleeps.

Yon marble minstrel's voiceless tone,
  In deathless songs shall tell,

When many a vanquished age hath flown,
  The story how he fell;
Nor wreck, nor change, nor winter's blight,
Nor time's remorseless doom,
  Shall dim one ray of holy light
That gilds your glorious tomb.

A Battle Call to Kentucky—1861.

Mary Walker Meriwether.

Arouse thee, Kentucky! the graves of thy sires
  Are pressed by the foot of the foe!
Has terror or aavrice smothered the fires
  That were wont in thy bosom to glow?

Arise! shall the voice of Virginia in vain
  Call aloud to the child of her pride?
Thou shouldst rush like a storm over mountain and
    plain
  To conquor or die at her side.

Alas! shall the rifles thy forefathers bore
  Hang, rusted and cold, in their place?
Has the spirit that kindled their bosoms of yore
  Forever deserted their race?

Awake, there is scorn in the beautiful eyes
  Of thy maidens and mothers and wives.
"Have we given," they ask, with indignant surprise,
  To cowards our loves and our lives?"

Awake and redeem us!   Arise in your might,
Or forfeit to manhood the claim.
The arm that refuses to strike for the right,
Let it wither and perish in shame.

And he who would hasten to cringe and to crawl
At the feet of the ruthless invader
A spirit so base it were flattery to call
A craven, a serf, or a traitor!

WESTERN DIXIE.

BY MRS. VIRGINIA SMITH.

Come along, boys, we'll go off to the wars.
Never mind the times, we'll all march cheerily.
Yo ho! yo ho! yo ho! in Dixie!
We'll talk about the girls round thebright camp fire.
Heave a little sigh and then sing merrily
Yo ho! yo ho! yo ho! in Dixie

CHORUS—We're bound to fight for Dixie.
Yo ho! yo ho!
Then shout hurrah for Dixie, boys!
We'll conquer now or never.

The Cairo boys talk mighty fine
About where they'd sup and where they'd dine,
Yo ho! yo ho! yo ho! in Dixie.
And they swelled like toads as the snake draws nigh,
And talked very loud 'bout the Fourth of July.
Yo ho! yo ho! yo ho! in Dixie!

Hurrah for the boys of Arkansas!
They'll bring Montgomery and Lane to taw.
Yo ho! yo ho! yo ho! in Dixie!

They'll show them what we rebels do.

They'll make the trip right through and through.
　　　Yo ho! yo ho! yo ho! in Dixie.
　　A battle fought, a battle won;
　　McCulloch's work has now begun.
　　　Yo ho! yo ho! yo ho! in Dixie!
　　And Woodruff's gallant little band
　　Was just in time to take a hand.
　　　Yo ho! yo ho! yo ho! in Dixie!

　　Missouri feels in further danger;
　　The will be freed by the rebel "Ranger."
　　　Yo ho! yo ho! yo ho! in Dixie!
　　Our troops will rise like the swelling tide
　　And sweep her borders far and wide,
　　　Yo ho! yo ho! yo ho! in Dixie!

GEN. MARMADUKE'S REPORT.

HEADQUARTERS 4TH DIV., CORPS T. M. D., }
　　BATESVILLE, ARK., Jan. 18, 1863. }

COLONEL:—In obedience to instructions from
Major-General Hindman, I marched from Lew-
isburg, Ark., December 31, 1862, via Yellville,
Ark., to strike the enemy in "rear and flank,"
with 1,600 men under Shelby, and 270 men under McDonald. Before marching I telegraphed
to Lieutenant-General Holmes, if it would not
be best to move up the troops under Colonel

White to co-operate in the movement. to which he consented and the order was given. Colonel Porter with 600 men moved forward for this purpose.

En route in the Boston Mountains, Shelby attacked 60 tories and deserters—killed 12, captured 27.

McDonald surprised, captured and burned Fort Lawrence, on Beaver Creek, Mo.—of its garrison.

Shelby captured and burnt the fort at Ozark. The garrison fled.

With Shelby and McDonald I attacked Springfield, Mo., after eight hours hard fighting, driving the Yankees before me into their strongholds. I captured one piece of artillery, a stockade fort, a large part of the town, which the Yankees burned as they retired. At night the fighting ceased. The Federal force there was 4,200. My loss was twenty killed and eighty wounded. Federal loss much greater. I did not deem it best to renew the attack. Next day marched toward Rolla. The Federals fled before me. I burned the forts at Sand Springs and Marshfield. After passing through Marshfield. formed a junction with Porter. After joining Porter. I march southeasterly. making my way toward Arkansas. At Huntsville I met. fought, and drove in the direction of Lebanon 1,600 infantry and 500 cavalry under General Merril. The battle was desperate; my loss was 15 killed and 70 wounded; of the former was the brave McDonald, Lieutenant-Colonel Weimer, Major Keitley and other brave officers and men. The Federal loss was also heavy; they sent in a flag to bury their dead.

I reached here to-day. Both men and horses need rest. I will forward detailed report.

Respectfully,

J. S. MARMADUKE,
Brigadier-General Commanding.

To Col. R. C. Newton, Chief of Staff, 1st Corps, T. M. Army.

JAMES W. JACKSON WHO FELL AT ALEXANDRIA.

JACKSON was asleep in the second story. Ellsworth entered his house (about day-break) and proceeded to the roof to take down the flag. The servant who aroused him told him the house was full of Lincoln men, and that some of them had gone up after the flag. and begged him not to leave his room. He rose immediately, and dressing himself in haste, seized his double-barrel shotgun, and had reached the first turn in the stairway leading to the third story when he met Ellsworth coming down with the flag wrapped around him and followed by a number of Zouaves. Without uttering a word Jackson shot him, the load carrying a part of the flag, like a piece of patching, into the heart itself, where it was afterward found.

One of the Zouaves fired almost the same instant upon Jackson, who was standing a little below and looking up at the stairway. The ball of the Zouave struck him just between the eyes, on the bridge of the nose, and passed out at the back of his head. In the very article of death he returned the fire of his enemy, as he was falling, but without effect. the load was buried in in the wall above his head.

LINES ON THE DEATH OF MAJ. HALL S. McCONNELL.

[Inscribed to his mother and sisters.]

BY MATTIE LEWIS.

He has fallen, the patriot, brother and son,
The pride of his comrades. He who to victory led on
His true noble followers, his country to save,
Is filling in glory a brave soldier's grave.
No voice of affection or kindred was near
To comfort the heart that in life knew no fear;
No soft hand to wipe from his marble pale brow
The death dew when he felt that departure is now.

> Ah! no; but his memory
>   By the brave and the free,
> Is cherished too fondly
>   Forgotten to be.

Never more will the sound of his rallying voice
In words of command that made freeman rejoice
Be heard high above the battle's wild roaring;
Never more for the fearless, proud spirit is soaring
In regions of mysteries above mortal ken
Where kindred and comrades shall meet him again:
His fame cannot die; but in song and in story
Will the name of McConnell be covered with glory.

> Ah! yes; for his memory
>   Remembered by me,
> Is cherished too fondly
>   Forgotten to be.

A "War Time" Letter From Mrs. Emily Maffitt to Mrs. Virginia Woodward, of Little Rock.

CLARKSVILLE, ARK., Aug. 9th. 1862.

DEAR SISTER—I have hunted the place over for a pen; and now I am writing with one that has been thrown away for years; and it may be you will not get to read this before the "Feds" get to read it. We heard they were trying to take Little Rock.

I am very busy spinning me some dresses. If I had enough chain I would weave some for you, but I have only enough for Orie and I. I can spin my six cuts easy and when I get my "hand in" can spin seven cuts. If the "Feds" don't get up this far and destroy what few clothes I have for Sunday, and I once get a start, I shan't ask anybody any odds—if I only had something to color with; but I intend to do like the rest, get bark and pine and cedar tops and parsley. I have about half a pound of log_wood but I don't intend everybody to know that or I would be. tormented to death. Virge, is there anything like indigo at Little Rock? If there is and I could get two ounces I would be glad. I am lucky in having cards, two-thirds of the people haven't cards; they are in a bad fix, some with large families. I will en-quire around and see if I can get some jeans for you, but I expect it will be a difficult matter to get cotton stripes for dresses. Doctor hired him some flannel spun and wove. I furnished the chain and the lady the wool and she spun and wove it for a dollar per yard. The prices are awful, four dollars a yard for jeans cloth. I intend to spin all I can. Would like to see you but I reckon we'll have to wait patiently until the war is over.

Mr. Breckinridge's Acceptance of the Richmond Nomination.

Hon. John Erwin, President of the Richmond Convention, has received the following letter from Hon. J. C. Breckinridge, accepting the nomination of that convention:

Lexington, July 26th, 1860.

In answer to your letter of 26th ult., containing official information of my nomination for the Presidency of the United States, by the Democratic Convention assembled at Richmond, I have to say that I accept the nomination, a shall strive to merit the confidence implied by the action of the convention. I trust that a full discussion of existing issues will result in establishing the Constitution and Union of the States upon immovable foundations.

John C. Breckenridge.

The Platform that Breckinridge and Lane Stand Upon.

Resolved, That the platform adopted by the Democratic party at Cincinnati be affirmed with the following explanatory resolutions:

1. *Resolved*. That the government of a territory, organized by an act of Congress, is provisional and temporary: during its existence all

i.—10

citizens of the United States have an equal right to settle with their property, in the territory, without their rights of either person or property being destroyed or impaired by congressional or territorial legislation.

2. *Resolved*, That it is the duty of the Federal government in all its departments to protect, when necessary, the rights of persons and property in the territories, and wherever else its constitutional authority extends.

3. *Resolved*, That when the settlers in a territory having an adequate population form a State Constitution, the rights of sovereignty commences, and being consummated by admission into the Union, they stand on an equal footing with the people of other states, and the state thus organized ought to be admitted into the Federal Union, whether its constitution prohibits or recognizes the institution of slavery.

4. *Resolved*, That the Democratic party are in favor of the acquisition of the Island of Cuba on such terms as shall be honorable to ourselves and just to Spain at the earliest practical moment.

5. *Resolved*, That the enactments of state legislatures to defeat the faithful execution of the fugitive slave law, are hostile in character, subversive of the constitution, and revolutionary in their effects.

6. *Resolved*, That the Democracy of the United States recognize it as the imperative duty of this government to protect the naturalized citizen in all his rights, whether at home or in foreign lands, to the same extent as its native born citizen.

AND WHEREAS, One of the greatest necessities of the age, in a political, commercial, postal and military point of view, is a speedy communication between the Pacific and Atlantic coasts. therefore, be it

Resolved, That the democratic party do hereby pledge themselves to use every means in their power to secure the passage of some bill to the extent of the constitutional authority of Congress for the construction of a Pacific railroad from the Mississippi river to the Pacific ocean, at the earliest practical moment.

A platform just to the North, just to the South, just to the East and just to the West, clearly defining the equality of the states and rights of all under the Constitution, as expounded by the Supreme Court, and they nominated Breckinridge and Lane as the standard bearers of the national Democracy.

Ho! For Breckinridge and Lane.

By Chas. C. Reed.

Huzzah! Huzzah! for Breckinridge,
　Kentucky's proudest son,
The noblest work of Liberty
　"That e'er the sun shone on."
March in the bands of "equal rights"
　For Breckinridge and Lane;
Upon our flag shall be,
"Equality and Equal Rights,"
　The banner of the free.

How a Texas Girl Writes.

It has been said here that some of our Texas soldiers who are in Arkansas have become dissatisfied and some have come home. I hope that the great body of the troops are firm and true. If the appeal of a girl would be heeded, I would say to them: Dear friends, do not desert your post. You have suffered, endured hardships; but endure a while longer. If subjugated, think of the fate of the Southern women. Think of your mothers, sisters, wives and sweethearts, and be firm. Here in Fannin County the women have not been idle. The women of Texas have spun, woven and made up clothing, besides contributing in every possible way to the comfort and welfare of the soldiers. If, instead of depending on the speculators. who bring goods and sell them at 500 per cent. the government would furnish us with thread at a fair price, we could make ample supplies of clothing. Since last summer I have made 172 yards of cloth, and if I could get thread would make as much more. In our way and with our means, we are fighting the great battle for liberty, and do not despond or grow impatient. for in good time God will give us peace and independence. I do not believe I have a relative so lost to honor as to desert so glorious a cause as ours in this. the most critical and trying time. Think. my friends, that the fate of those you love: the fate of civil and religious freedom: the hope of the world and the glory of our beautiful country. are in your hands. Be not recreants. but be men —brave men, true men, patient men and heroes.

Respectfully.

A. L. J. BOMBARGER.

Fannin County. Texas.

STONEWALL JACKSON'S BOYS IN CAMP.

It is when idle in camp that the soldier is a great institution, yet one that must be seen to be appreciated. Pen can not fully paint the air

of cheerful content, care, hilarity, irresponsible
loungings, and practical spirit of jesting that
"obtains," ready to seize on any odd circumstance in its licensed levity. A "cavalry-man"
comes rejoicing in immense top boots, for which,
in fond pride, he has invested full forty dollars
of pay. At once the cry of a hundred voices
follow him along the line: "Come up out'er
them boots! Come out! Too soon to go into
winter quarters! I know you're in there! See
your arm stickin' out." A bumbkin rides by
in an uncommonly big hat, and is frightened at
the shout: "Come down outer that hat; come
down. 'Tain't no use to say you ain't up thar!
I see your legs hanging out." A fancy staff
officer was horrified at the irreverent reception
of his nicely twisted moustache as he heard from
behind innumerable trees: "Take them mice
out of your mouth. No use saying they ain't
there; I saw their tails sticking out." Sometimes a rousing cheer is heard in the distance.
It is explained: "Boys, look out! Here comes
old Stonewall!"

LINES.

BY A VOLUNTEER.

Do not think that the volunteer selfishly pines
  At the hardships that fall to his share;
Do not think that his heart for one moment resigns
  The sad thought of home sorrows and care.

Oh! 'tis not in the fierce tide of conflict alone
  That our freedom and rights have been won—
To each warrior's grasp comes a woman's low moan,
  Whose faint echo no soldier would shun.

Are there no weary fingers and no aching heads
  Toiling long for the brother in camp?
Are there no hapless families left to vague dreads
  Of the approach of stern penury's tramp.

Are there no homeless mothers or wives in despair
  Drifting down upon poverty's stream?
What brave man with such sufferings at home would com-
     pare
  His own trials though hard they may seem?

Though the sentinal couches beneath the rude storm,
  And more lightly encases the old tattered blanket around
     his shivering form;
Yet he thinks not alone of the cold,
  He can brace up his nerves to withstand the rude blast.

But he trembles again at the sigh
  That comes home to his ear, as each wild gust sweeps
     past,
Bringing anguish his heart tells him why.
  'Mid the fierce clash of arms, when a grave seems to
     yawn

  'Neath the feet as he presses the foe,
For one moment his eye dims for those who may mourn

Weary years after he is laid low.
Though his soul aches with grief as he leaves his canteen

With a comrade whose life's reed is broke,
By that chain on the dying man's breast he has seen
That two hearts have been rent by the stroke.

PORT HUDSON, LA., April 14, 1863.

THE name of Patrick Cleburne of the Confederate army is one which should not be forgotten in the military annals of our race. He was the hero of over thirty pitched battles, and the number of minor actions in which he participated is beyond precedent. He was distinguished for decision, and almost every movement committed to his division was successful. He received the incessant congratulation of the Southern press, and was complimented by the Confederate congress. After the death of Jackson, he got the soubriquet of "The Stonewall of the South." For he was to the army of Tennessee what Jackson was to that of Virginia. But most of all, he was tender and generous to the vanquished, and as Ferguson says, "Kindly Irish to the Irish." He lies in a lonely grave in the village of Columbia. Tennessee, whither he was borne after the battle of Franklin by one of his officers. History will not consign his name to oblivion. This leaflet to his memory,

Cleburne.

How far and fast the autumn blast
  Beats the dead leaves o'er the ground;
As fast and far as the hand of war
  Strewed our country's brave around!
And their nameless graves are the ocean's caves,
  The forest and the mountain glen,
Where the vulture screams and the angry streams
  Are hiding the bones of men!
        And what anguished cries
        From the South arise,
      From the brave ones fallen in vain?
        While the victor North
        Sings pæans forth,
      And exults in her broad domain!

As fire suppressed in Vesuvius' breast,
  The latent fires of crime
In the human frame pulse on the same
  Till fanned by the storms of time;
As the lava fold swept uncontrolled
  Where Pompeii's glories shone,
So the wakened rage of a vandal age
  When freedom is overthrown!
        And we'll look in tears,
        Through long long years.
      For the brightness shrouded oe'r,
        But the golden rays
        Of our halcyon days
      Shall return to the land no more!

But I sing of one whose glory shone
  Like a meteor, bright and grand,
Who gave his name to the trump of fame
  And his blood to a generous land.
        The festive toast,

The soldier's boast,
The type of a martial age!
The foe of wrong,
The soul of song,
And the light of a future page.

The base grow bold for the power of gold,
The vain through fear of scorn,
The good wax strong in their hate of wrong,
But he was a warrior born.
From his eagle glance and stern "Advance!"
And his action swift as thought,
The rank and file from his own fair ilse
Their courage electric caught,
As the whirlwind's path
Shows its fiercest wrath,
Through the lordliest forest pines,
So the deepest wave
Of the fallen brave
Told where Cleburne crossed the lines.

On Richmond's plain his captive train
Outnumbered the host he led,
And he won his stars on the field of Mars
Where the glorious Johnson bled!
'Twas his to cope while a ray of hope
Illumed his flag—and then
'Twas his to die while that "flag flew high "
In the van of chivalric men!
Nor a braver host
Could Erin boast,
Nor than he a more gallant knight,
Since the peerless Hugh
Crossed the Avon dhu,
And Bagnal's hosts aflight.

There were friends afar who watched your star
As it rose with the Southern cross,

There were hearts that bled when its course was
   sped
  And old Ireland felt your loss!
While her flowers blow or her waters flow
  Through Shannon Suir and Lee.
The patriot's song shall roll along
  Their winding waves for thee!
       And they'll tell with pride
       How Cleburne died
    In the land of the free and brave,
       How his sword of might
       Was a beam of light,
    Though it led to an exile's grave.

DEAD ON MANASSAS PLAIN.

BY J. AUGUSTINE SIGNIAGO.

Close beside the broken grasses,
  Near the setting of the day,
On the plain of red Manassas,
  Low a Northern soldier lay;
And his comrades all were flying
  Fast before their Southern foes.
He was wounded, and was dying,
  Where the wild grass thickly grows.

Far away from every brother,
  He was dying all alone—
And the thoughts of home and mother
  Made him shudder, sigh and moan—
When a wounded Southerner spied him,
  And, forgetting they were foes,
Dragged himself, with pain, beside him,
  And gave comfort to his woes.

There the Southerner was kneeling,
  Praying on his native sod—
For the dying man appealing
  To the mercy of their God,
And while they could smell the slaughter
  Of that bloody battle scene,
Gasped the dying man for water,
  And drank from his foe's cateen.

Fast the Northerner was straying
  To that bright and better land;
Still the Southerner was praying,
  And they pressed each other's hand,
Once more gazed at one another,
  Once more pointed overhead,
Once more breathed the name of mother,
  And the Northerner was dead.

All Over Now.

All over now! The trumpet blast,
  The hurried tramping to and fro,
The sky with battle smoke o'ercast,
  The flood of death and woe.

All ended now! The syren song
  Of hope's estatic lay is hushed,
And minor chords, in plaintive tones,
  Wail out when gayer notes are crushed.

'Neath feathery snow, in hallowed ground,
  By far Potomac's rippling stream,
Our loved ones sleep. The lulling waves
  Can ne'er disturb the soldier's dream.

Then whisper "Peace"—the dove of peace,
  Like Noah's, searches for her nest.
She folds her wings among the dead,
  But with the living finds no rest!

All over now! We gave our all—
  Our loved ones, home and prayers.
God willed that we awhile should wait,
  In bitterness and tears.

What need of tears? Why must they flow
  When all but life and breath are gone?
God help us all!—and help the heart
  To murmur still, "Thy will be done."

And Heaven those heartfelt tears doth take
  Upon a cloudlet's breast
And bear them to the distant field,
  Where the soldier lies at rest,

And pour them on the cloud as dew
  Upon the hero slain,
That he no more unwept may lie
  Upon the distant plain.

When falls the soldier brave,
  Dead at the feet of wrong,
The poet sings, and guards his grave
  With sentiment of song.

Go, songs! he gives command!
  Keep faithful watch and true—
The living and the dead of the conquered land
  Have now no guards save you.

And ballads, mark ye well,
  Thrice holy is your trust.
Go out to the fields where warriors fell,
  And sentinel the dust.

An Old Battlefied in Georgia.

By Frank L. Stanton.

The softest whisperings of the scented South,
And rust and roses in the cannon's mouth;
And where the thunders of the fight were born,
The wind's wild tenor in the tinkling corn;
With songs of larks, low lingering in the loam,
And blue skies bending over love and home—
And far away somewhere upon the hills,
Or where the vales ring with the whip-poor-wills
Sad, wistful eyes, and breaking hearts that beat
For the loved sound of unreturning feet;
And when the oaks their leafy banners wave,
Dream of the battle and an unmarked grave.

Freedom and Right.

By John W. Hoodward.

O, say, not believe not the gloom of the grave
   Forever has closed upon Freedom's glad light,
Or sealed are the lips of the honest and brave,
   Or the scorners of baseness are robbed of their right;
Though the true to their oaths into exile are driven,
   Or weary with wrong with their own hands have given
Their blood to their foes and their spirits to Heaven,
   Yet immortal is Freedom—immortal is Right!

Let us not be by partial defeats disconcerted,
   They will make the grand triumphs more signal and
         bright;
Thus whetted, our zeal will be double exerted,

And the cry be raised louder of Freedom and Right!
For these two are one, and they mock all
  Of despots their holy alliance to sever.
Where there's Right be sure there are Freeman, and ever
  Where Freeman are found, God will prosper the Right.

And battle they still where the voice of earth's sorrow
  Tells of wrongs to avenge, and oppressors to smite;
And conquerors to-day, or conquered to-morrow,
  Fear ye not in the end they will conquer outright—
Oh! to see the bright wreath round the victor brows
      shining,
  The laurel and bay in their green folds entwining
The German oak-leaf and Shamrock combining,
  And above them our flag in the breeze and the light!

There are sore, aching bosoms, and dim eyes of weepers,
  Will be gathered to rest e'er that day sees the light;
But ye, too, will hallow the graves of the sleepers,
  The blest ones, we owe to them Freedom and Right!
Fill your glasses meanwhile: To the hearts that were true,
      boys!
  Who had wrongs to redress, but won right for you, boys;
Drink to them! to the Right! to the Freedom and Right!

The Memorable Month.

The month of April, 1865, will stand memorable in our history above all other periods of time.   Here are the leading events:

April 1—Sheridan's victory at Five Forks.

April 2—The grand assault at Petersburgh.

April 3—Occupation of Richmond.

April 6—Sheridan routes Lee's forces.

April 9—Lee surrenders to Grant.

April 12—Our forces occupy Mobile.

April 14—Assassination of President Lincoln.

April 15—Andrew Johnson becomes President.

April 16—Battle of Columbus, Georgia, last fight of the war.

April 19—Funeral of the President at Washington.'

April 26—Death of the assassin Booth.

April 26—Surrender of General Johnston's army.

The Band in the Pines.

[Heard after Pellham died.]
BY JOHN ESTON COOKE.

Oh! band in the pine woods cease!
  Cease with your splendid call;
The living are brave and noble,
  But the dead were the bravest of all.

They throng the martial summons
  To the loud triumphant strain,
And the dear bright eyes of long dead friends
  Come to the heart again.

They come with the ringing bugle,
  And the deep drum's mellow roar,
'Till the soul is faint with longing
  For the hand we clasp no more.

Oh! band in the pine wood cease!
  Or the heart will melt in tears,
For the gallant eyes and smilling lips,
  And the voices of old years.

"Oh! death, thou pleasing end of human woe,
Thou cure for life, thou greatest good below;
Still may'st thou fly the coward and the slave,
And thy soft slumbers only bless the brave."

My Soldier Boy.

I am dreaming, ever dreaming of a silver-sanded shore,
Where the blue waves softly murmur as they roll forever-
  more,
Where the sunbeams brightly glowing kiss the wavelets as
  they flow,
And the scented breeze is sighing where the orange flowers
  blow,
'Till the music of the waters with their cadence low I hear
As it mingles with the sighing breeze and falls upon my
  ear;
And I seem to breathe the odors that are wafted from that
  shore
Where my heart is fondly turning, fondly tnrning ever
  more.

I.—11

When the sunset melts in glory and the daylight softly
    dies
'Till the purple twilight deepens and o'er all in splendor
    lies,
When nor voice nor sound is heard save the whisperings
    of the breeze
As evening chants her vespers low among the leafy trees,
As I watch the golden hues that fade and vanish from my
    sight
Like the hopes and dreams of vanished years when lost in
    gloomy night—
More glorious is the sunset fancy pictures on that shore
Where my heart is fondly turning, fondly turning ever-
    more.

Do you ask why I am dreaming, ever dreaming of that
    shore?
Why the music of its waters seems to haunt me evermore?
There encamped are Southern heroes, beside that mur-
    muring sea,
And a soldier boy among them whose name is dear to me-
Who with that gallant hero band, in his country's hour of
    of need,
When danger threatened, at her call resolved to save or
    bleed;
And there beside that murmuring sea their white tents do,
    the shore
Where my heart is fondly turning, fondly turning ever-
    more.

When the tranquil earth is dreaming in the soft embrace
    of night,
And the quiet stars are keeping holy watch upon each
    height;
When angel eyes upon us seem a gentle watch to keep,
While some are wrapt in slumbers light—some are left to
    weep;

Then by that camp stand sentinels the solemn midnight
    round,
And my soldier boy is keeping watch, or slumbering on the
    ground;
I am praying Heaven to guard from ill that silver-sanded
    shore
Where my heart is fondly turning, fondly turning ever-
    more.

                     —T. E. GRAYSON.

Near Benton, Miss., Oct., 1861.

ON THE DEATH OF GENERAL "STONEWALL" JACKSON.

The leaf has perished in the green,
   And while we breath beneath the sun,
   The world, which credits what is done,
Is cold to all what might have been.

Hide your sweet faces, beautiful flowers;
Forget me! forget me! bright blooming bowers;
Steal away! steal away! glowing sunbeams,
We can not bear you now—for sorrow's dark dreams
Had ne'er pictured true the grief that will rest
Forever, and aye, in a proud nation's breast.
O, hush birdling! hush your joyous lay,
And cease brooklet, cease! your song is too gay—
For why will you joy and beauty now bring,
When merciless death hath wintered our spring?
   The hero is gone!

Morn for him! morn for him!—best of the brave.
Scatter ye love garlands over his grave;
Aged and young, soldiers, lover and friend,

Anthems of praise with your requiems blend—
Praise for the greatness that praise leaves untold.

Quietly weep, ne'er the life that is cold!
A nation's sad heart in comfortless woe
Be the death-knell tolling soft, sweetly and low.
  Jackson is gone!
                    —LILLIAN ROSELL MESSENGER.
TUSCUMBIA, ALA., May 13, 1863.

JOHN PELHAM.

[KELLEY'S FORD, March 17, 1863.]

Just as the spring comes laughing through the strife,
  With all its gorgeous cheer,
In the bright April of historic life,
  Fell the great cannoneer.

The wondrous lulling of a hero's breath
  His bleeding country weeps—
Hushed in the alabaster arms of death,
  Our young Marcellus sleeps.

Nobler and grander than the child of Rome,
  Curbing his chariot's steeds—
The knightly action of a Southern home
  Dazzled the land with deeds.

Gentlest and bravest in the battle brunt,
  The champion of the truth,
He bore his banner to the front
  Of our immortal youth.

A clang of sabres 'mid Virginia snow,
  The fiery pang of shells,
And there's a waft of immortal woe
  In Alabama dells.

The pennant droops that lead the sacred band
  Along the crimson field;
The meteor blade sinks from the nerveless hand
  Over the spotless shield.

We gazed and gazed upon that beauteous face,
  While round the lips and eyes,
Couched in their marble slumber, flashed
  The grace of a divine surprise.

O Mother of a blessed soul on high!
  Thy tears may soon be shed.
Think of thy boy, with princes of the sky,
  Among the Southern dead.

How must he smile on this dull world beneath,
  Fevered with swift renown.
He, with the martyr's amaranthine wreath
  Twining the victor's crown!

JAMES R. RANDALL.

MY WIFE AND CHILD.

BY HENRY R. JACKSON.

The tattoo beats, the lights are gone,
  The camp around in slumber lies.
The night with solemn pace moves on;
  The shadows thicken o'er the skies,
But sleep my weary eyes hath flown,
  And sad, uneasy thoughts arise.

I think of thee, oh, dearest one
  Whose love my early life hath blest,
Of thee and him, our baby boy,
  Who slumbers on thy gentle breast;
God of the tender, frail and lone,
  Oh, guard the tender sleeper's rest.

Now, while she kneels before Thy throne,
　Oh, teach her, Ruler of the Skies,
That while by Thy behest alone
　Earth's mightiest powers fall or rise,
No tear is wept to Thee unknown,
　No hair is lost, no sparrow dies;

That Thou canst stay the ruthless hand
　Of dark disease, and soothe its pain;
That only by Thy stern commands
　The battle's lost, the soldier's slain;
That from the distant sea or land
　Thou bring'st the wanderer home again.

Whatever lot may fate bestow,
　Loved with a passion almost wild,
By day, by night, in joy or woe,
　By fears oppressed or hopes beguiled,
From every danger, every foe,
　Oh, God, protect my wife and child.

STONEWALL JACKSON'S DEATH—THE LAST HOURS OF HIS LIFE.

The spring of 1862 saw a large Federal army assembled on the north bank of the Rappahannock, and, on the first of May, General Hooker, its commander, had crossed and firmly established himself at Chancellorsville. General Lee's forces were opposite Fredericksburg, chiefly a small body of infantry only watching the upper fords. This latter was compelled to fall back before General Hooker's great force, stated by Major-General Price, of the United States army, in the New York *Herald*, to the number of 159,300 men, and Lee hastened, by forced marches, from Fredericksburg to Chancellorsville, to check the further advance of the enemy. This was on May 1, and the Confederate advance force, under Jackson, on the same evening, attacked General Hooker's intrenchments facing towards Fredericksburg. They were found impregnable, the dense thickets having been converted into abattis, and every avenue of approach defended with artillery. General Lee, therefore, directed the assault to cease, and consulted with his corps commanders as to further operations, Jackson suggested a rapid movement around the Federal front and a determined attack upon the right flank of General Hooker, west of Chancellorsville. The ground on his left and in his front gave such enormous advantages to the Federal troops that an assault there was impossible, and the result of the consultation was the adoption of Jackson's suggestion to attack the enemy's right. Every preparation was made that night, and on the morning of May 2 Jackson set out with Hill's, Rhodes' and Colston's divisions, in all 22.000 men, to accomplish his undertaking. Chancellorsville was a single brick house of large dimensions. situated on the plank road from Fredericksburg to Orange. and all around it were the thickets of the country known as the Wilderness.   In this tangled undergrowth the Federal works had been thrown up. and such was the denseness of the woods that a column moving a mile or two to the south was not apt to be seen.   Jackson calculated upon this. but fortune seemed against him.   At the Catherine Furnace, a mile or two from the Federal line. his march was discovered and a hot attack was made on his rear guard as he moved past.   All seemed now discovered, but. strange to say, such was not the fact.   The Federal officers saw him plainly, but the winding road which he pursued chanced here to bend towards the south, and it was afterward discovered that General Hooker supposed him to be *in full retreat upon Richmond*.   Such at last was the statement of Federal officers.   Jackson repulsed the attack upon his rear, continued his march and. striking into what is called the Brook road, turning the head of his column northward, and rapidly advanced around General Hooker's right flank.   A cavalry force under General Stuart had moved in front and on the flanks of the column, driving off scouting parties and other too inquisitive wayfarers; and, on reaching the junction of the Orange and

Germanna roads, a heavy Federal picket was forced to retire. General Fitz. Lee then informed Jackson that, from a hill near at hand, he could obtain a view of the Federal works, and, proceding thither, Jackson reconnoitered. This reconnoisance showed him that he was not far enough to the left, and he said briefly to an aid, "Tell my column to cross that road," pointing to the plank road. His object was to reach the old turnpike, which ran straight down into the Federal right flank. It was reached at about 5 o'clock in the evening, and, without a moment's delay, Jackson formed the line of battle for an attack. Rhodes' division moved in front, supported, at an interval of two hundred yards, by Colston's, and behind these A. P. Hill's division marched in column, like the artillery, on account of the almost impenetrable character of the thickets on each side of the road. Jackson's assault was sudden and terrible. It struck the Eleventh corps, commanded on this occasion by General Howard, and completely surprised them; they retreated in confusion upon the heavy works around Chancellorsville. Rhodes and Colston followed them, took possession of the breastworks across the road, and a little after 8 o'clock the Confederate troops were within less than a mile of Chancellorsvile, preparing for a new and a more determined attack.

Jackson's plan was worthy of being the last military project conceived by that resolute and enterprising intellect. He designed putting his entire force into action, extending his left and placing that wing between General Hooker and the Rappahannock. Then, unless the Federal commander could cut his way through, his army would be captured or destroyed. Jackson commenced the execution of this plan with vigor and an obvious determination to strain every nerve and incur every hazard to accomplish so decisive a success. Rhodes and Colston were directed to retire a short distance and re-form their lines, now greatly mingled, and Hill was ordered to move to the front to take their places. On fire with his great designs, Jackson then moved forward in front of the troops toward Chancellorsville; and there and then the bullet struck him which was to terminate his career. The details which follow are given on the authority of Jackson's staff officers, and one or two others who witnessed all that occurred. In relation to the most tragic portion of the scene, there remained, as will be seen, but a single witness. Jackson had ridden forward on the turnpike to reconnoitre and ascertain, if possible, in spite of the darkness of the night, the position of the Federal lines. The moon shone, but it was struggling with a bank of clouds, and afforded but a dim light. From the gloomy thickets on each side of the turnpike, looking more weird and sombre in the half light, came the melancholy notes of the whippoorwill. ``I think there must have been ten thousand,'' said General Stewart afterwards. Such was the scene amid which the events now about to be narrated took place. Jackson had advanced, with some members of his staff, considerably beyond the building known as ``Melzi Chancellor's,'' about a mile from Chancellorsville, and had reached a point nearly opposite an old dismantled house in the woods near the road, whose shell-torn roof may still be seen. when he reined in his horse and remained perfectly quiet and motionless, listened intently for any indications of movements in the Federal lines. They were scarcely two hundred yards in front of him, and seeing the danger to which he exposed himself, one of his staff officers said: `` General, don't you think this is the wrong place for you?'' He replied quickly, almost impatiently: `` The danger is all over, the enemy is routed. Go back and tell A. P. Hill to press right on.'' The officer obeyed, but had scarcely disappeared when a sudden volley was fired from the Confederate infantry in Jackson's rear, and on the right of the road, evidently directed upon him and his

escort. The origin of this fire has never been
discovered, and after Jackson's death there was
little disposition to investigate an occurrence
which occasioned bitter distress to all who by
any possibility could have taken part in it. It
is possible, however, that some movement of
the Federal skirmishers had provoked the fire;
if this is an error, the troops fired deliberately
upon Jackson and his party under the impression that they were a body of Federal cavalry reconnoitering. It is said that the men
had orders to open on any object in front,
"especially upon cavalry," and the absence of
pickets or advance force of any kind on the
Confederate side explains the rest. The enemy
were almost in contact with them; the Federal
artillery, fully commanding the position of the
troops, was expected to open every moment,
and the men were just in that excited condition
which induces troops to fire at any and every
object they see. Whatever may have been the
origin of the volley, it came, and many of the
staff and escort were shot and fell from their
horses. Jackson wheeled to the left and galloped into the woods to get out of range of the
bullets, but he had not gone more than twenty
steps beyond the edge of the turnpike, in the
thicket, when one of his brigades drawn up
within thirty yards of him fired a volley in

their turn, kneeling on the right knee, as the flash of the guns showed, as though prepared to "guard against cavalry." By this fire Jackson was wounded in three places. He received one ball in his left arm, two inches below the shoulder, shattering the bone and severing the chief artery; a second passed through the same arm below the elbow and the wrist, making its exit through the palm of the hand; a third bullet entered through the palm of his right hand, about the middle, and passing through, broke two bones.

At the moment when he was struck he was holding his rein in his left hand, and his right was raised either in the singular gesture habitual to him at times of excitement, or to protect his face from the boughs of the trees. His left hand immediately dropped at his side, and his horse no longer controlled by the rein, and frightened by the firing, wheeled suddenly and ran from the fire in the direction of the Federal lines. Jackson's helpless condition now exposed him to a very distressing accident. His horse ran violently between two trees, from one of which a horizontal bough extended, at about the height of his head, to the other, and as he passed between the trees this bough struck him in the face, tore off his cap, and threw him violently back on his horse. The blow was so violent as to nearly unseat him, but it did not do so, and rising erect again he caught the bridle with the broken and bleeding fingers of his right hand, and succeeded in turning his horse back into the turnpike. Here Capt. Wilburn of his staff succeeded in catching the reins and checking the animal, who was almost frantic with terror, at the moment when, from loss of blood and exhaustion, Jackson was about to fall from the saddle. The scene at this time was gloomy and depressing. Horses mad with fright at the close firing were seen running in every direction, some of them riderless, others defying control, and in the wood lay many wounded and dying men. Jackson's whole party, except Capt. Wilbourn and a member of the signal corps, had been killed, wounded or dispersed. The man riding just behind Jackson had his horse killed; a courier was wounded, and his horse ran into the Federal lines; Lieut. Morrison, aid-de-camp, threw himself from the saddle, and his horse fell dead a moment afterwards; Capt. Howard was wounded and carried by his horse into the Federal camps; Capt. Leigh had his horse shot under him; Capt. Forbes was killed, and Capt. Boswell, Jackson's chief engineer, was shot through the heart, and his dead body carried by his frightened horse into the lines of the enemy near at hand. Such was the result of the causeless fire. It had ceased as suddenly as it began, and the position in the road which Jackson now occupied was the same from which he had been driven. Capt. Wilbourn, who, with Mr. Wynn of the signal corps, was all that was left of the party, noticed a singular circumstance which attracted his attention at this moment. The turnpike was utterly deserted with the exception of himself, his companion and Jackson, but in the skirting of thicket on the left he observed some one sitting his horse by the side of the road and coolly looking on, motionless and silent. The unknown individual was clad in a dark dress, which strongly resembled the Federal uniform, but it seemed impossible that he could have penetrated to that spot without being discovered, and what followed seemed to prove that he belonged to the Confederates. Captain Wilbourn directed him to "ride up there and see what troops those were"—the men who had fired on Jackson—when the stranger slowly rode in the direction pointed out, but never returned with any answer. Who this silent personage was, is left to conjecture. Captain Wilbourn, who was standing near Jackson, now said, "They certainly must be our troops," to which the general assented by a nod of the head, but said nothing. He was looking up the road toward his lines, "with apparent astonishment," and continued for some time to look in that direction, as if unable to realieze he could have been fired upon and wounded by his own men. His wound was bleeding profusely, the blood streaming down so as to fill his gauntlets, and it was necessary to secure assistance promptly. Capt. Wilbourn asked him if he was much injured, and urged him to make an effort to move his fingers, as his ability to do this would prove that his arm was not broken. An effort which his companion made to strengthen it caused him great pain, and, murmuring, "You had better take me down," he leaned forward and fell into Captain Wilbourn's arms. He was so much exhausted by loss of blood that he was unable to take his feet out of the stirrups, and this was done by Mr. Wynn. He was then carried to the side of the road and laid under a small tree, where Captain Wilbourn supported his head, while his companion went for a surgeon and an ambulance to carry him to the rear, receiving strict instructions, however, not to mention the occurrence to any one but Dr. McGuire, or another surgeon. Captain Wilbourn then made an examination of the general's wounds. Removing his field glasses and haversack, which latter contained some paper and envelopes for dispatches, and two religious tracts, he put these on his person for safety, and, with a small pen-knife, proceeded to cut away the sleeves of the india-rubber overall, dress coat, and two shirts from the bleeding arm. While this duty was being performed, General Hill rode up with his staff, and, dismounting beside the general, ex-pressed his great regret at the accident. To the question whether his wound was painful, Jack-son replied, "Very painful," and added that his "arm was broken." General Hill pulled off his gauntlets, which were full of blood, and his sabre and belt were also removed. He then seemed easier, and, having swallowed a mouth-ful of whisky which was held to his lips, appeared much refreshed. It seemed impossible to move him without making his wound bleed afresh, but it was absolutely necessary to do so, as the enemy was not more than 150 yards dis-tant, and might advance at any moment, and all at once a proof was given of the dangerous position which he occupied. Captain Adams, of Gen-eral Hill's staff, had ridden ten or fifteen yards ahead of the group, and was now heard calling out: "Halt; surrender! Fire on them if they don't surrender!" At the next moment he came up with two Federal skirmishers, who had at once surrendered with an air of astonishment, declaring that they were not aware that they were in the Confederate lines. General Hill had drawn his pistol, and mounted his horse, and he now returned to take command of his line, and advance, promising Jackson to keep his accident from the knowledge of the troops, for which the General thanked him. He had scarcely gone when Lieutenant Morrison, who had come up, reported the Federal lines advancing rapidly, and then within about a hundred yards of the spot, he exclaimed: "Let us take the General up in our arms and carry him off." But Jackson said faintly, "No; if you can help me up, I can walk." He was accordingly lifted up, and placed upon his feet, when the Federal batteries in front opened with great violence, and Captain Leigh, who had just arrived with a letter, had his horse killed under him by a shell. He leaped to the ground near Jackson, and the latter, leaning his right arm on Captain Leigh's shoulder, slowly dragged himself along towards the Confederate lines, the blood from his wounded arm flowing profusely over Captain Leigh's uniform. Hill's lines were now in motion to meet the coming attack, and, as the men passed Jackson, they saw from the number and rank of his escort that he must be a superior officer. "Who is that—who have you there?" was called; to which the reply was, "Oh, its only a friend of ours, who is wounded." These inquiries be-

came, at last, so frequent that Jackson said to
his escort: "When asked. just say it is a Confederate officer." It was with utmost difficulty
that the curiosity of the troops was evaded.
They seemed to suspect something, and would
go around the horses, which were led along on
each side of the General to conceal him, to see
if they could discover who it was. At last one
of them caught a glimpse of a.man who had lost
his cap, as we have seen in the woods, and was
walking bareheaded in the moonlight, and suddenly the man exclaimed in the most pitiful
tones, says an eye witness: "Great God; that
is General Jackson!" An evasive reply was
made, implying that this was a mistake, and the
man looked from the speaker to Jackson with a
bewildered air, but passed on without further
comment. All this occurred before Jackson
had been able to drag himself more than twenty
steps; but Captain Leigh had the litter at hand,
and, his strength being completely exhausted,
the General was placed upon it, and borne toward the rear. The litter was carried by two
officers and two men, the rest of the escort
walking beside it and leading the horses.
They had scarcely began to move, however, when the Federal artillery opened a
furious fire upon the turnpike from the
works in front of Chancellorsville, and a hurri-

cane of shell and canister swept down the road.
What the eye then saw was a scene of disordered troops, riderless horses and utter confusion. The intended advance of the Confederates had doubtless been discovered, and this
fire was directed along the road over which they
would move. By this fire Generals Hill and
Pender with several of their staff were wounded,
and one of the men carrying the litter was shot
through both arms and dropped his burden.
His companion did likewise, hastily flying from
the dangerous locality, and but for Captain
Leigh who caught the handle of the litter it
would have fallen to the ground. Lieutenant
Smith had been leading his own and the General's horse, but the animals now broke away
in uncontrollable terror and the rest of
the party scattered to find shelter. Under
these circumstances the litter was lowered
by Captain Leigh and Lieutenant Smith
into the road, and those officers lay down by it
to protect themselves in some degree from the
heavy fire of artillery, which swept the turnpike
and " struck millions of sparks " from the flinty
stones of the roadside. Jackson raised himself
up on his elbow and attempted to get up, but
Lieutenant Smith threw his arm across his
breast and compelled him to desist. They lay in
this manner for some minutes without moving,

the hurricane still sweeping over them. "So far as I could see," wrote one of the officers, "men and horses were struggling with a most terrible death." The road was otherwise deserted. Jackson and his two officers were the sole living occupants of the depot. The fire of the canister soon relaxed, though that of shot and shell continued, and Jackson rose to his feet. Leaning on the shoulders of the party who had rejoined him, he turned aside from the road, which was again filling with infantry, and struck into the woods, one of the officers following with the litter. Here he moved with difficulty among the troops, who were lying down in line of battle, and the party encountered General Pender, who had just been slightly wounded. He asked who it was that was wounded, and the reply was "a Confederate officer." General Pender, however, recognized General Jackson, and exclaimed: "Ah, General, I am sorry to see you have been wounded. The lines here are so much broken I fear we will have to fall back." These words seemed to affect Jackson strongly. He raised his head and said, with a flash of the eye: "You must hold your ground, General Pender! You must hold your ground, sir!" This was the last order Jackson ever gave upon the field.

His strength was now completely exhausted,

and he asked to be permitted to lie down upon
the ground. But to this the officers would not
consent. The hot fire of the artillery, which
still continued, and the expected advance of
the Federal infantry, made it necessary to move
on, and the litter was again put in requisition.
The General, now nearly fainting, was laid upon
it, and some litter bearers having been procured, the whole party began to move through
the tangled wood toward Melzi Chancellor's.
So dense was the undergrowth and the ground
so difficult their progress was very slow. An
accident now occasioned Jackson untold agony.
One of the men caught his foot in a vine, and,
stumbling, let go of the litter, which fell heavily
to the ground. Jackson fell upon his left
shoulder, where the bone had been shattered,
and his agony must have been extreme. "For
the first time," says one of the party, "he
groaned, and that most piteously." He was
quickly raised, however, and a gleam of moonlight passing through the foliage overhead revealed his pale face, closed eyes and bleeding
breast. Those around him thought that he was
dying. What a death for such a man! All
around him was the tangled wood, and half
illumined by the struggling moonbeams; above
him burst the shells of the enemy, "exploding,"
says an officer, "like showers of falling stars,"

and in the pauses came the melancholy notes of
the whippoorwills borne on the night air. In
this strange wilderness the man of Port Republic and Manassas, who had led so many desperate
charges, seemed about to close his eyes and die.
But such was not to be the result then. When
asked by one of the officers whether he was
much hurt, he opened his eyes and said quietly,
without further exhibition of pain: "No, my
friend, don't trouble yourself about me." The
litter was then raised upon the shoulders of the
men, the party continued its way, and reaching
an ambulance near Melzi Chancellor's, placed
the wounded General in it. He was then borne
to the field hospital at Wilderness Run, some
five miles distant.

Here he lay throughout the next day, Sunday, listening to the thunder of the artillery
and the long roll of the musketry from Chancellorsville, where Stuart, who had succeeded
him in command, was pressing General Hooker
back towards the Rappahannock. His soul
must have thrilled at that sound long familiar,
but he could take no part in the conflict. Lying
faint and pale in a tent in rear of the " Wilderness Tavern," he seemed to be perfectly re-
signed, and submitted to the painful probing of
his wounds with soldierly patience. It was ob-
viously necessary to amputate the arm, and one

of his surgeons asked, "If we find amputation necessary, shall it be done at once?" To which he replied with alacrity, "Yes; certainly, Dr. McGuire, do for me whatever you think right." The arm was then taken off and ne slept soundly after the operation, and on waking began to converse about the battle. "If I had not been wounded," he said, "or had had one more hour of daylight, I would have cut off the enemy from the road to United States Ford; we would have them entirely surrounded, and they would have been obliged to surrender or cut their way out; they had no other alternative. My troops may sometimes fail in driving an enemy from a position, but the enemy always fails to drive my men from a position." It was about this time we received the following letter from General Lee: "I have just received your note informing me that you were wounded. I cannot express my regret at the occurrence. Could I have directed events, I should have chosen for the good of the country to have been disabled in your stead. I congratulate you upon the victory which is due to you skill and energy." The remaining details of Jackson's illness and death are known. He was removed to Guinea's Depot, on the Richmond and Fredericksburg railroad, where gradually he sank, pneumonia having attacked him. When told that his men on Sunday had advanced upon the enemy shouting, "Charge and remember Jackson!" he exclaimed, "It was just like them! it was just like them! They are a noble body of men. The men who live through this war," he added, "will tell, 'I was one of the Stonewall brigade' to their children." Looking soon afterwards at the stump of his arm, he said, "Many people would regard this as a great misfortune. I regard it as one of the great blessings of my life." He subsequently said, "I consider these wounds a blessing, they were given me for some good and wise purpose, and I would not part with them if I could." His wife was now with him and when she announced to him, weeping, his approaching death, he replied with perfect calmness, "Very good, very good, it is all right." These were nearly his last words. He soon afterwards became delirious and was heard to mutter, "Order A. P. Hill to prepare for action!" "Pass the infantry to the front!" "Tell Major Hawks to send forward provisions for the men!" Then his martial ardour disappeared, a smile diffused itself over his pale features, and he murmured, "Let us cross over the river and rest under the shade of the trees!" It was the river of death he was about to pass, and soon after uttering these words he expired. Such are the circum-

stances which attended the last hours of the
soldier who had so long carried the Southern
standard, and accomplished such extraordinary
successes. With his disappearance from the
scene the fortunes of the South like her banner
began to droop. The Federal forces were often
driven back thereafter but were never completely defeated. Great leaders were left, but
their exertions appeared to secure no definite
results. Jackson had passed away, by an in-
scrutable decree of the Almighty, and no one
seemed able to fill his place.—VIRGINIA COR-
RESPONDENCE OF THE NEW YORK WORLD.

LAST WORDS OF STONEWALL JACKSON.

BY D. S. MORRISON.

"Let us cross over the river and rest under the shade of
the trees."

"Over the river," a voice meekly said,
Whose clarion tones thousands had obeyed,
As in ranks upon ranks they grandly rushed on
To battle for liberty, country and home.

"Over the river," immortality's plains,
In verdure eternal where peace ever reigns,
Rejoice with their beauty his vision of faith,
As the spirit approaches the river of death.

" Over the river," oh! glorious sight,
An escort celestial awaits with delight,
In the glittering armor of glory arrayed,
They welcome him over to rest in the shade.

"Over the river," no more to command
The drum beat to arms in a war-stricken land;
No bugle call summons the brave to the fray,
No squadrons leap forth in battle array.

"Over the river," now a heavenly guest,
'Neath the shades of the trees forever at rest;
His memory and fame to ages belong,
And his lofty deeds live in story and song.
NEW ORLEANS, 1865.

THE BURIAL OF LIEUTENANT-GENERAL JACKSON.

(A Dirge.)

[Shortly after the lamented death of the great
Stonewall Jackson, the following dirge appeared in the Richmond *Whig*, from the pen
of A. W. Kercheval, Esq., of Virginia, written to the music of "Oporto," the Portuguese
hymn of the Nativity, a tune which had been
appropriated by the Virginia troops for the
burial of their dead.]

Comrades, advance! Your colors draped with mourning.
    Muffled your drums, and arms reversed, ye brave.
Trumpets blow dirges for the great commander,
    Ye follow gallant Jackson to his grave.

Muskets, fire clear, your iron throats peal thunder
  O'er him who oft victorious legious led;
Commemorate ye still the great commander,
  As volley answers volley o'er him dead."

Bands now strike up your noblest martial music,
  Light lie the turf on his heroic breast,
While fair hands strew *immortelles* o'er him fallen—
  Oh, emblems pure and holy of his rest!

Close up the ranks, O brothers, all!
  And feel each heart throb nearer,
The bravest at our side must fall,
  The living are the dearer,
Yet pause a moment in the strife
  To drop the tear of sorrow.

In October, 1894, Captain James Earwood, of
Clarksville, Ark., organized a company. With
a company, under Captain James Garrett, on a
raid through the mountains north of Clarksville, they were fired upon from ambush by a
scouting company of Federals. .

Captain Earwood and Lieutenant Davis were
instantly killed. First Lieutenant Watts took
command, charged the enemy and they were
put to flight. Returning to the spot they were
fired upon. He, with Robt. Jackson, Abe Miller, Will Mann, and other young comrades, took
the lifeless bodies of Lieutenant Davis and Cap-

tain Earwood on their saddles, carried them a distance of ten miles to Clarksville for burial. They secretly dug the grave of Captain Earwood at the risk of their being captured or shot in the enemy's lines, and the body of the brave soldier was left with a few neighbor women, who proffered to assist in the ceremony of burial. Such was a soldier's life in those perilous days in Arkansas.

IN MEMORY OF CAPTAIN JAMES EARWOOD.

In a quiet valley in Arkansas
  You may find that lonely grave,
In rain and sunshine always
  Where unkept grasses wave.

At the twilight hour he was buried,
  In haste, almost in sight of the foe,
By Southern women, with gentle hands,
  So tenderly—their faces pale with woe.

They shaped the earth above him,
  Without funeral dirge or psalm,
Just a sob from mourning hearts
  To break the evening's calm.

No voice of prayer has hallowed
  That brave soldier's place of rest,
No minister of God hath blest it
  And yet it hath been blest.

For, in faith and hope, that little band
  Looked up from the blood-stained sod
To a home above, where angels dwell,
  Among the blest of God.

—ROBIN REID.

CLARKSVILLE, ARK.

David Dodd, of Askansas.

By Fannie Borland.

Who knew what passed in those long years,
    In Arkansas?
Who cared to mark the falling tears
    Of Arkansas?
We know of many hero graves
Where not one wreath of laurel waves,
And not one stone a hearing craves
    In Arkansas.

Thermopylæ is far away
    From Arkansas,
And knew of heroes ere the day
    Of Arkansas.
Leonidas did hold the pass
Till men fell thick as summer grass
And *one* did read that in his class
    In Arkansas.

Rome was held full many a sea
    From Arkansas,
But we read the story of the *three*
    In Arkansas.
And *one* did read it every day
And heard above his comrades' play
Strange voices call him far away
    From Arkansas.

And when close by his college door
    In Arkansas
He stood a mighty crowd before
    In Arkansas.
He knew his lessons all were done,
Yet was beneath the Southern sun.
A lesson taught to many a one
    In Arkansas.

He did not urge his youth's fair claim
    On Arkansas,
Nor tell a single comrade's name,
    Oh, Arkansas!
He would not take a length of days
That led through such dishonored ways.
Better a grave than blighted bays,
    Oh, Arkansas!

He looked beyond the foeman's fire
    To Arkansas.
He saw his comrades' camping fire in Arkansas!
He marked each form, *unfettered*, strong;
He heard them singing loud and long,
And half way broke into that song
    Of Arkansas.

He saw his sister's eyes grow dim
    In Arkansas,
With watching long and late for him
    In Arkansas.
He saw his brother at the door
Look far across to the river shore.
He would not see them any more
    In Arkansas.

Free breezes in his hair did play
    In Arkansas.
And he might be as free as they
    In Arkansas.
Only a few short words to say,
He looked up brightly to the day.
Heaven is not far away
    From Arkansas.

He did not hold Thermopylæ,
    Oh, Arkansas!
Nor help to hew the bridge away,

                    Oh, Arkansas!
            But the little hero held his tongue
            And heard the death knell round him rung,
            And saw the rope above him swung,
                    Oh, Arkansas!

            Who knew what passed in those long years
                    In Arkansas,
            Or darkened history with the tears
                    Of Arkansas?
            And yet among each fairer State,
            Who weeps his individual fate
            Can one a grander tale relate
                    Than Arkansas?
Memphis, Tenn., October 16, 1868.

CONFEDERATE DEAD AT GETTYSBURG.

BY ISAAC F. EATON.

The armies they had ceased to fight,
    The night was still and dark,
And many thousands on the field
    Were lying stiff and stark.
The stretcher men had come along
    And gathered all they could.
A hundred surgeons worked that night
    Behind the clump of wood.

They flashed the lanterns in my face,
    As they went hurrying by;
The sergeant looked, and said, "He's dead,"
    And I could not reply.
The bullet had gone through my breast;
    No wonder I was still.
But once will I be nearer death
    Than when upon that hill.

A gray-clad picket came along,
  Upon his midnight beat.
He came so near me that I tried
  To move and touch his feet.
Instead, he bent and felt my breast,
  Where life still fought at bay.
No one who loved me could have done
  More than this man in gray.

Chilled with damp of blood and dew,
  His blanket o'er me spread.
A crimson sheaf of wheat he brought,
  A pillow for my head.

*   *   *   *

The sounds of war are silent now
  We call no man our foe
But soldier hearts cannot forget
  The scenes of long ago.
Dear are the ones who stood with us
  To struggle or to die;
No one can oftener breathe their names
  Or love them more than I

*   *   *   *

But from my life, I'd give a year
  That gray-clad man to see;
To clasp in love the foeman's hand
  Who saved that life to me

Little Giffen of Tennessee.
By Frank O. Tichnor.

Out of the focal and foremost fire,
Out of the hospital walls as dire!
Smitten of grapeshot and gangrene
(Eighteenth battle, and he sixteen!)
Specter, such as you seldom see,
"Little Giffen of Tennessee."

"Take him and welcome!" the surgeon said;
"Little the doctor can help the dead."
So we took him and brought him where
The balm was sweet in the summer air,
And we laid him down on a wholesome bed—
Utter Lazarus from heel to head!

And we watched the war with bated breath,
Skeleton boy against skeleton death;
Months of torture, how many such?
Weary weeks of stick and crutch,
And still a glint of the steel blue eye
Told of a spirit that *wouldn't die.*

And didn't; nay, more, In deaths despite,
The crippled skeleton learned to write.
"Dear Mother," at first, of course, and then
"Dear Captain," inquiring about the men.
Captain's answer: "Of eighty and five,
Giffen and I are left alive."

Word of gloom from the war one day,
Johnson pressed at the front they say.
Little Giffen was up and away;
A tear, his first, as he bade good-by
Dimmed the glint of his steel blue eye,
"I'll write, if spared." There was news of the fight,
But none of Giffen. He did not write.

I sometimes fancy, that were 1 a king
Of the princely Knights of the Golden Ring—
With the song of the minstrel in mine ear,
And the tender legend that trembles here,
I'd give the best on his bended knee,
The whitest soul of my chivalry
For " Little Giffen of Tennessee."

Fellow Feeling in the Army.
The Boy in Gray.

The day after the battle of Fredericksburg
Kershaw's brigade occupied Mary's Hill, and
Syke's division lay one hundred and fifty yards
ahead, with a stone wall between the two forces.
The intervening space between Syke's men and
the stone wall was strewn with dead, dying and
wounded Union soldiers, victims of the battle
of the day before. The air was rent with
groans and agonizing cries of "Water! water!"
"General," said a boy sergeant in gray, "I can't
stand this." "What is the matter, sergeant?"
asked the general. "I can't stand hearing those
wounded men crying for water. May I go and
give them some?" "Kirkland," said the general, "the moment you step over the wall you'll
get a bullet through your head; the skirmish-
ing has been murderous all day."

"If you'll let me I'll try it."

"My boy, I ought not to let you run such a risk, but I cannot refuse. God protect you; you may go."

"Thank you, sir." And with a smile on his bright, handsome face, the boy sergeant sprang over the wall, down among the sufferers, pouring the water down their parched throats. After the first few bullets, his Christ-like errand became understood, and shouts instead of bullets rent the air. He came back at night to his bivouac untouched.

An Incident of Battle.—The Boy in Blue.

By Mrs. May M. Anderson.

A drummer boy fell in the heat of battle,
  Only a lad in a suit of gray;
He heard the shouts and the musketry rattle
  Over the field where the wounded lay.
No one could help while the guns were raking
  Meadow and wood with their leaden hail.
"The foe has charged and our lines are breaking;
  "The day is lost," was his bitter wail.

He closed his eyes while the shock and thunder
  Of awful carnage was opened anew,
Then fainted away; was it any wonder,
  When another bullet had pierced him through?
He roused at last and the tide of battle
  Again had changed, for he heard the fray
In the wood beyond with the ceaseless rattle
  Of shot and shell in their deadly play.

His lips were parched and his throat was burning;
  "O, for some water," he faintly sighed;
He heard at his feet the labored turning
  Of a prostrate form, while a clear voice cried,
"My canteen's full but my arms are broken,
  See, you can reach if you bend this way;"
He moved and groaned, and with thanks unspoken,
  Reached for the water, then shrank away.

He saw with a start and a sudden quiver,
  The youth at his feet wore a suit of blue,
And he marked the frown and the creeping shiver
  Which mastered and held him and thrilled him
    through,
At sound of the yell from the rebel forces,
  Which told the tale that the fight was done—
To the Southern lad how the fresh life courses
  Along his veins, for the fight is won!

"See here is water!" the youth had rallied,
  And moved still nearer the form in gray.
It cost him much, for his face grew pallid;
  He gasped, yet struggled to faintly say,
"I'd reach you the can but my arms are shattered,"
  Then closed his eyes in a death-like swoon.
He had given his all to a foe, what mattered,
  When all would be ended so swift and soon?

With a sob in his throat for the hero before him,
  The drummer boy turned, and with tremulous
    touch
On the pale face sprinkled the water, and o'er him
  Murmered a prayer. That was all; not much.
Not much, yet methinks when the sorrow and
  anguish
  For soldier and drummer boy ended that night,
Mid horrors around where faith seemed to languish,
  The darkness was spanned by a rift of light.

A Southern Exile.

A Letter from Hon. Jacob Thompson, of Mississippi.

Dublin, Aug. 11, 1866.

To Captain Wm. Delay:

My Dear Sir—Your interesting letter of the 16th ult. was received by me on yesterday, and the only way in which I can manifest the unqualified pleasure it gives me is by making you an immediate reply.

I never knew, until I was cast out an exile, without home or country, and, apparently, without friends, how necessary to human happiness is human sympathy. A stranger in a strange land, caring for nobody, nobody caring for me, I determined, for my pleasure and improvement, to visit the principal scenes of historic interest, and thus familiarize myself with the story of those who had gone before me. I went to Paris (which, take it all in all, is the pleasantest city in the world), and there remained until I could re-read her history and learn something of the French language. Then I went to Switzerland and visited the retreats of the different distinguished exiles, who, in the violence of party, had been driven from their country to this place of quiet and safety. I went to Rome, the home of the greatest men and purest patriots, whose history adorns the annals of the past, and there I remained two months, industriously employed all the time in examining the ruins of former greatness and grandeur, never feeling the slightest interest in the living, so absorbed with thoughts, principles and actions of the mighhty dead. Then I went to the delightful city of Naples—delightful for its climate and situation, not for its people; here was the seat of royalty now in banishment. Then to Egypt, the cradle of letters and learning; then to Palestine, to tread the ground our Savior trod; to see the places at which he performed his glorious works; to climb the sides of Mount Olivet; to stand on Mount Calvary; drink the waters from the pool of Siloam, and gaze upon the tomb where they laid his body, which could only retain it for its appointed time. From here I think I came away a better man. I returned through the Greek Isles. of vast interest to the student; up the Adriatic to Venice—a most singular place, with a most marvelous history; thence through Vienna, Munich, Frankfort, Cologne, Brussels, to Paris again. Here Mrs. Thompson left, yearning to see the land we both loved, and love still; but I could not go with her.

ASHES OF GLORY.

BY A. J. REQUIER.

Fold up the gorgeous silken sun,
  By bleeding martyrs blest,
And heap the laurels it has won
  Above its place of rest.

No trumpet's note need hardly blare,
  No drum funeral roll,
Nor trailing sables drape the bier
  That frees a dauntless soul!

It lived with Lee and decked his brow
  From Fate's empyreal palm;
It sleeps the sleep of Jackson now,
  As spotless and as calm.

It was outnumbered, not outdone,
  And they shall shuddering tell
Who struck the blow its latest gun
  Flashed ruin as it fell.

Sleep, shrouded ensign—not the breeze
  That smote the victor tar
With death across the heaving seas
  Of fiery Trafalgar;

Not Arthur's knights amid the gloom,
  Their knightly deeds have starred;
Not Gallic Henry's matchless plume,
  Nor peerless born Bayard.

Not all that antique fables feign,
  And orient dreams disgorge;
Nor yet the silver cross of Spain,
  And Lion of St. George,

Can bid thee pale!   Proud emblem still,
  Thy crimson glory shines
Beyond the lengthened shades that fill
  Their proudest kingly lines.

Sleep in thine own historic night,
  And be thy blazoned scroll;
A warrior's banner takes its flight
  To greet the warrior's soul.

THE EARL OF DERBY TO GENERAL LEE.

[On the fly-leaf of the copy of the Iliad given by the late
  Earl of Derby to General Lee]:

The grave old bard who never dies
  Receive him in our native tongue;
I send thee, but with weeping eyes,
  The story that he sung.

Thy Troy has fallen; thy dear land
  Is marred beneath the spoiler's heel;
I cannot trust my trembling hand
  To write the grief I feel.

Oh, home of tears!   But let her bear
  This blazon to the end of time;
No nation rose so white and fair,
  None fell so pure of crime.

The widow's moan, the orphan's wail,
  Are around thee; but in truth be strong;
Eternal right, though all things fail,
  Can never be made wrong.

An angel's heart, an angel's mouth,
  (Not Homer's) could alone for me
Hymn forth the great Confederate South—
  Virginia first, then Lee.

Humor in Camp.

The admiration for Stonewall Jackson was by no means confined to his own section. The Federal prisoners always expressed a great desire to see him, and some loudly cheered him. This was particularly the case at Harper's Ferry, where the whole line of 11,000 prisoners greeted him with lusty shouts. Citizens say that the hostile troops always spoke of him in terms of unqualified praise.

A gentlemen in the Valley of Virginia relates that when Fremont and Shields thought that they had entrapped him beyond the possibility of escape, Sigel's Dutch soldiers passed his house crying, "Shackson in a shug!" (jug), "Shackson in a shag!" And when they returned from Port Republic, when asked what they had done with Jackson; "By tam, the stopper came out of the shug. If the rebels don't make him de President, Sigel's men will make him."

"He'll See When He Wakes."

By Frank Lee.

[In one of the battles of Virginia a gallant young Mississippian had fallen, and at night, just before burying him, there came a letter

from his betrothed. One of the burial group
took the letter and laid it upon the breast of the
dead soldier with the words: "Bury it with
him. He'll see when he wakes."]

Amid the clouds of battle smoke
  The sun had died away,
And where the storm of battle broke
  A thousand warriors lay.
A band of friends upon the field
  Stood 'round a youthful form,
Who, when the war-cloud's thunder pealed,
  Had perished in the storm.
Upon his forehead, on his hair,
  The coming moonlight breaks,
And each dear brother standing there
  A tender farewell takes.

But ere they laid him in his house
  There came a comrade near,
And gave a token that had come
  From her the dead held dear.
A moment's doubt upon them pressed,
  Then one the letter takes,
And lays it upon his breast,
  " He'll see it when he wakes."
O, thou, who dost in sorrow wait,
  Whose heart with anguish breaks,
Though thy dear message came too late,
  "He'll see it when he wakes."

No more amid the fiery storm
  Shall his strong arm be seen,
No more his young and manly form
  Tread Mississippi's green;
And e'en thy tender words of love—
  The words affection speaks—

Come all too late—but oh! thy love
  " Will see them when he wakes."
No jars disturb his gentle rest,
  No noise his slumber breaks,
But thy words sleep upon his breast,
  " He'll see them when he wakes."

How the Soldiers Talk.

By Joseph Scrutchen, of Atlanta, Ga.

We have heard the Yankees yell,
  We have heard the Rebels shout,
We have weighed the matter well,
  And we mean to fight it out.
In victory's happy glow,
  In the gloom of utter rout,
We've pledged ourselves, " Come weal or woe,"
  By Heaven! to fight it out!

'Tis now too late to question
  What brought the war about,
'Tis a thing of pride and passion,
  And we mean to fight it out.
Let the " big wigs" use the pen,
  Let them caucus—let them spout—
We've half a million weaponed men,
  And mean to fight it out.

Our dead and loved are crying
  From many a stormed redoubt,
In swamps and trenches lying,
  "Oh! comrades, fight it out.
'Twas our comfort as we fell

To hear your gathering shout,
Rolling back the Yankee yell,
God speed you, fight it out."

The negro, free or slave,
We care no pin about,
But for the flag we gave,
We mean to fight it out.
And while that banner brave,
One Yankee flag shall flout,
With rallying arm and flashing glare,
By Heaven, let's fight it out.

Oh, we've heard the Yankees yell,
We have heard the Rebels shout,
We have weighed the matter well,
And mean to fight it out.
In the flash of perfect triumph,
And the gloom of utter rout,
We have sworn on many a bloody field,
We mean to fight it out.

MRS. WINFIELD SCOTT'S KINDNESS.

DR. JOHN F. KENNEDY was surgeon of the Fourteenth Mississippi Regiment of the Confederacy. He was captured at Fort Pillow, and sent to Camp Chase, Chicago. On reaching Chicago, he was met by a messenger. who, he afterward learned, was sent by Mrs. General Scott, and was conducted to one of the best hotels in the city. The next morning at the breakfast table he found under his plate three hundred dollars, all in gold, with a note in a lady's handwriting telling him to live well, as he should have all the money he wished. The note was signed " Rebel Sympathizers." He was placed on duty in the hospital in which sick Confederates were confined. He soon formed the acquaintance of a noble chivalric soldier, Col. W. S. Hawkins, Colonel of a Tennessee regiment, who had been installed as a nurse in the same hospital. Colonel Hawkins was nursing a fellow prisoner who was engaged to be married to a most beautiful young lady. She proved faithless, and her letter came breaking the troth soon after the prisoner died. Colonel Hawkins sent the following reply:

> Your letter came, but came too late,
>   For Heaven had claimed its own.
> Ah! sudden change from prison bars
>   Unto the great white throne.
> And yet I think he would have stayed
>   For one more day of pain,
> Could he have read those tardy words
>   Which you have sent in vain.

WILSON CREEK.

COL. C. P. HYDE, of Virginia, in reference to the famous battle of Wilson Creek. the first great battle of the Trans-Mississippi department: " I, too, was there in Colonel Clarkson's regiment, Colonel Weightman's brigade, Gen. James S. Rains, Second Division, M. S. G.. at which place the beloved Weightman was killed. Captain Bledsoe belonged to our division, and clear and high above the din of musketry could be heard 'Old Sacramento' dealing death to the enemy while our infantry made charge after charge over a bald prairie knob, only to be cut down by the enemy that was concealed in a depression among the post-oak runners in front of us. Captain Bledsoe's three gun battery was stationed upon an eminence in our rear and fired over our heads. Here in front of us the lamented General Lyon fell, with his famous gray horse. There is a mystery surrounding this memorable battle. It will be remembered that the Missouri State troops, under General Price, from Southwest Missouri, and the Confederate forces from Texas and Arkansas—from Northern Arkansas under General Ben McCullough—were united before the Wilson's Creek battle, and it was said there was some contention between the two generals as to who should take command. Be that as it may, General McCullough assumed command and issued orders to the army to be in readiness to march at 9 p. m. August 9, as we supposed, to invest Springfield, about ten miles distant, at which place General Lyon was camped with the Federal army. We did not march as ordered. Why not? History has it that McCullough resolved to march on to Springfield, but postponed the attack on account of a storm. The facts are there was no rain and no storm, but it was cloudy and dark. We lay on our arms, as it were, all night, without further orders. At day-break, while some of us were asleep, others up, with camp fires, warming cold grub, we were surprised by one of our command, who came in, breathless, with the news that the Feds were just over the hill. We supposed him mistaken and were teasing him about getting scared, but before the laugh was over we were attacked in front and rear almost simultaneously, and not a company in line. Then for five long hours that sea of humanity was lashed with fury. At one time, when one mad billow seemed ready to engulf the frail bark in front, it would be rolled back by the fury of the storm, and thus the ebb and flow of that human sea continued, until the fury of the storm had spent its force. General Lyon had fallen, General Sigel routed and his command demoralized. The retreat of the Federal forces left the Confederates master of the field. After the fury of this sanguinary conflict had subsided, the spectacle was heart-rending. Hundreds of both sides lay pale in death, while hundreds lay writing in pain, weltering in gore, under a mid-day August sun. I have been in many hard-fought battles—Lexington, Mo., Praire Grove, Elkhorn Tavern, Jenkins' Ferry, etc., but never saw such heroism displayed as on that day. I was senior Captain nearly three years in Mitchell's (the Eighth Missouri) infantry—Frost's old brigade—and was in all the important engagements of the Mississippi, but have never seen Oak Hill or Wilson Creek battles equaled in ferocity and heroism.

———

[THE above account of the battle of "Oak Hill" (Wilson Creek) calls to mind a little incident of an officer who did brave fighing during the battle—Col. J· E. Cravens (Arkansas regiment). He was surprised while at his breakfast; sprang to his saddle, declaring he did not prefer his coffee, as it had been sweetened a little too much to his taste with grapeshot.]

———

AN old darkey tells the story of the battle: " I was dar, and me and some more white gemmen soldiers retreated till we got bout ten mile from de enimy, and den we drawed up a line of battle and swore we wan't gwine to retreat any furder."

GENERAL LEE AND TRAVELER.

REV. ROBT. TUTTLE, CISCO, TEXAS.

THE occasion of the following lines was a memorable picture of the battle of Spottsylvania Court House, Virginia, May 12, 1864. At one time during the engagement, General Lee stood by the head of "Traveler," his favorite horse. The position was one of danger, being right on the crest of the hill, not far from a one-story building, and near the outer edge of a small grove of trees. The writer was an eye-witness, and was deeply impressed with the General's splendid attitude:

Behold the horse!   A dappled gray!
I saw him in the month of May
When wild flowers bloomed about his feet
And sunshine was his mantle meet.

The shapely head he held up high
And fire seemed flashing from his eye;
Arched grandly, too, his neck and mane
And on them fell the slackened rein.

Down from the withers to the tail
The curve was perfect in detail;
While depth of chest, and haunch and side
Showed where his strength did most reside.

With limb and hoof and pasturn small
The body round and plump withal,
No pattern could be perfecter
Than was the form of "Traveler"

Rare model for an artist's skill,
For brush or chisel, or for quill,
For there with muscles strained and tense
His mould was sheer magnificence.

Bucephalus was not more gay
In ancient battle's stern array
Than was that grand Virginia gray
That mutely champed his bits that day.

A day of battle truly, then!
A day of death to many men!
For war a gory drama played,
But "Traveler" was undismayed.

Dismounted and quite near his head
The right hand to the halter wed,
His rider stood, bold leader he!
The great, the gallant, Robert Lee.

Broad-shouldered, tall, stout and straight,
The left hand down—his look sedate;
He wore a cap and suit of gray,
And gazed, but nothing had to say.

What courtiness in him was seen!
Aye, what nobility of mein!
As there Horatius-like he stood,
The honored, wise and great and good.

Great chieftains had preceded him
With cups of glory to the brim,
But he among them all was Prince,
Unrivaled in the past, or since.

The battle raged around him near;
The clash of arms he saw—could hear,
But dauntless he stood out to view,
Though deadly missiles round him flew.

Brave chief and charger, such were they,
And Dixie's hue of martial gray,
And such they will in memory be
While time and sense remains to me.

Immortal Spottsylvania!
'Twas on that sacred hill of thine
'Mid shouts of victory and huzzah
We saw this picture from the line.

Ye artists paint the signal scene,
Or fashion it in bronze, or stone,
That generations yet unseen,
In all Southland's sunny zone—

May look upon Lee's noble form
As there he stood amid the storm,
And did our Dixie boys command
Who fought for rights and home and land.

THE SWORD OF HARRY LEE.

BY JAMES D. McCABE.

An aged man, all bowed with years,
   Sits by his hearthstone old.
Beside him sits in reverend awe
   A youth all proud and bold.
He listens with rapt eagerness
   The old man's every word.
One aged hand rests on his knee,
   The other grasps a sword.

"My son," the gray-haired patriot said,
   "A precious legacy
I give into your keeping now,

The sword of Harry Lee.
I wore it through the fatal storm
That darkened o'er our sky,
When brave men died for liberty
To stand or nobly die!

"We prized our holy liberty,
  We hated tyranny;
We vowed we'd die as brave men die
  If we could not be free;
We swore eternal vengeance on
  Our foes from o'er the sea.
And night and day we bravely rode
  With 'Light Horse Harry Lee.'

"Ah! how we loved our noble chief!
  A hero grand was he.
No craven thought e'er filled the heart
  Of noble Harry Lee.
And where the fight was thickest, boy,
  We'd see his bright sword flash,
And the heavens would ring with his shout,
  As on the foe he'd dash!

"One day, it all comes back again,
  Though I am old and gray.
The battle had raged long and fierce,
  For we could not give way.
Our noble leader gave the word,
  And on the foe we flew,
Resolved to drive from off the field
  The base-born hireling crew.

"Our chieftain, at the legion's head,
  Rode on exultingly,
When a redcoat vile his musket raised
  To murder Harry Lee.
I dashed before the hero bold

Right in the deadly strife
And clove the base dog to the earth
And saved brave Harry's life.

"And when the fearful flight was o'er
　The major for me sent,
And I was led by Captain Carnes,
　That night into his tent.
He grasped my hand quite heartily.
　The flush was on his cheek,
And tears stood in his manly eyes—
　His voice was hoarse and weak.

"He thanked me for all I had done—
　I know his every word—
And then he took from round my waist
　My tried and trusty sword.
He said that I must give it him,
　For it had ne'er been raised
Save in the cause of liberty—
　With joy I was nigh crazed.

"He gave me his own trusty blade,
　That oft had led the free,
And told me I must wear it for
　The sake of Harry Lee.
Ah, boy, that was a happy night,
　For proud he might be,
Who e'er deserved such heartfelt praise
　From gallant Harry Lee.

"I wore this blade all through the war,
　And when the storm was o'er,
I kept it bright and free from rust,
　As in the days of yore.
And when the clouds came down again
　Upon our skies so bright,
I buckled on this blade again
　And wore it through the fight.

"And when the soft, sweet southern breeze,
 From tropic regions far,
Came laden with the clang of arms_
 And thrilling notes of war,
I took the old sword from its place,
 With tears of honest pride,
And buckled it all fiercely by
 Your gallant father's side.

"He bore it manfully and well,
 In regions far away;
It flashed o'er Palo Alto's plains
 And sunny Monterey;
It never was laid down in shame,
 God grant I ne'er may see
One base, foul blot upon the sword
 Of dear old Harry Lee!

"Now, boy, I draw this sword again—
 Alas! that it must be,
That I must count as foes the sons
 Of those who fought with me!
My limbs are old and feeble now,
 And silvery is my hair,
I cannot wield this sword and so
 I give it to your care.

"To-day I saw your noble chief,
 And ah! I seemed to see,
Erect again, before me stand
 The form of Harry Lee;
That same bright eye, that noble form,
 That bearing light and free;
Ah, yes, he's like his noble sire,
 This son of Harry Lee.

"I'm thankful, boy, he'll lead you on
 To the wild battle-field,

> For his father's heart within him beats,
>   And never will he yield;
> Stand by your General to the last,
>   Obey his every word,
> And yield your life before you dare
>   To yield his father's sword!
>
> "Now go and do your duty, boy,
>   You bear no craven's name,
> And as you dread your grandsire's curse,
>   Ne'er sully it with shame;
> And I, as long as life shall last
>   Within this bosom free,
> Will ask God's blessings on you, and
>   The son of Harry Lee."

FROM CAPTAIN RIDLEY'S JOURNAL.

APRIL 17-22.—I learn from a staff officer of
General Johnston that orders have been issued
to divide with the army all the silver coin in
possession of Johnston's paymaster—$54,000.
This will give each man $1.80 apiece, a small
sum for four years' trials and hardships, los of
treasures, blood and life. Just here, by way of
parenthesis, I got for my share $1.15—four
quarters, one dime and a five-cent piece. I gave
my faithful boy, Hannibal, the dime and five
cents, and brought my four quarters home and
had them fixed to hand down to posterity as
a kind of heirloom. I got a jeweler to send

them to New York and have engraved on them
my rank, when, where and to whom I surrendered, and the basis of negotiations between
Johnston and Sherman. The engraving cost
me $30.00. I gave them to a kinswoman to
keep for me. One day she wrote me in great
distress that a servant had stolen her purse, and
in it were the four quarters, the last I ever heard
of them. Oh, what would I give to find those
four silver coins.

HISTORY OF THE UNITED STATES.

BY PERCY GREG, AN ENGLISHMAN.

If Parliament had unjustly taxed the Americans, Congress by a northern majority had done
the same to South Carolina. The South had
been taxed from first to last for the exclusive
benefit of the North. It was a grand and
special grievance that the king had threatened
to raise the slaves against their masters. The
North had gone very far in that direction before
war began, and in war went further than
George III. If the colonies were entitled to
judge their own cause, much more were the
Southern States. Their rights, expressly de-
fined and solemnly guaranteed by law, had
been flagrantly violated; the compact which
alone bound them had beyond question been

systematically broken for more than forty years by the States which now appealed to it." The author quotes the memorable farewell speech of Jefferson Davis in the United States Senate as showing "the temper in which the Southern people dissolved the bonds of union, and prepared to stand alone in the midst of an unsympathetic and censorious world; to protect their own interests, and, if need. be, to defend their homes and families, their property and their rights, the honor and independence of their States to the last against five-fold greater than theirs," and "no nation," he adds, "ever challenged a dubious cause—appealed to the god of battles to make right compensate might, and courage prevail over numbers and resources, but with a clear consience. Assuredly none ever fought to the last, after hope had vanished, and when all was lost but honor, unless convinced in its inmost soul that divine justice if not divine providence was on its side. To say that the South seceded and fought for slavery is," Mr. Greg argues, "to accuse her of political imbecility," and to reply to the oft made allegation "that the desire to develop as well as preserve slavery was the very mainspring of secession," he points to the fact that the Constitution of the Confederate States absolutely and unconditionally prohibited the slave trade, as showing that the accusation is not only false, but the exact reverse of the truth. He pays frequent tribute to the courage of the Confederate soldier. Englishman though he be, of the charge of Pickett's division at Gettysburg he says; "The charge of the Light Brigade was less desperate and its trial far less prolonged. The bravest among the victors of Inkerman, of Albuera, of Worth and Gravelotte, might envy the glory of Pickett's defeat."

PELHAM AT FREDRICKSBURG.

At the battle of Fredricksburg, December, 1862, Major John Pelham, Chief of Stuart's Artillery, and then only eighteen years old, with one Parrot gun delayed the Federal advance for an hour, to give time for necessary manœuvers, fighting his gun in the face of the concentrated fire from the entire Federal artillery, as well as the musketry fire from their assaulting column. His gunners in this memorable action were Mississippi Frenchmen, and above the frightful din of battle could be heard the strains of their hymn, "The Marsellaise," sung by them as they worked their piece. Pelham's conduct on this occasion won the loftiest praise man has ever earned. Lee watching him, said, "It is glorious to see such courage in one so young." Such words from such a man!

Into the hurtling storm of shell.
Into the gaping mouth of hell,
  Pelham, the dauntless, lashed—
Out from the meager line of gray,
Out to the bloody fringe of fray,
  Where thousand thunders crashed.

Lashes to straining horses plied,
Cheers of defiance as they ride
  Under the eyes of Lee
Out of the day and into night,
Clouded in smoke they ride to fight—
  Glorious sight to see!

Out of that bedlam Freedom speaks;
Hear it in Pelham's Parrot's shrieks,
  Pelham, 'tis bravely done!
In the concentring deadly hail,
Daring to die but not to fail
  Pelham still fights his gun!

What is that sound? 'Tis not a cheer—
There, yet again—list! Comrades hear!
  Hark, 'tis the hymn of France!
Rising the lofty anthem swells,
Over the din of countless hells
  Freedom defiance chants!

Never was witnessed braver deed,
Bringing of praise its richest meed,
  Making a deathless name—
"Courage sublime in one so young!"
Words from the heart of Lee he wrung,
  Crown of immortal fame!
                    —A. SIDNEY MORTON.
St. Paul, Minn.

A STAR from the battle flag of the Twelfth
Mississippi Regiment, A. N. Va., has been
framed, and is treasured the more because of the
following lines written by Capt. Fred. J. V.
LeCand, the last adjutant of that regiment:

Only a piece of bunting; soiled by the weather and torn,
   Dirty, a term most contemptuous!—tattered and gone to
      decay:
Valueless save to the worthy who followed where it was
      borne;
   No charm to present to the many;   alas! it has served its
      day.

Its day was a time when heroes fought
Amid flashing of cannon, when the air was fraught
With the groans of the dying and cries of pain
Of thousands of soldiers who lay 'mong the slain.

Only a star, dim and fallen; a star fast fading from sight;
One of a fair constellation—lost in the darkness of night;
A star which forever has set, but whose history ever will
      tell
Of the deeds of the " boys in gray," who under its shadow
      fell.

My Little Volunteer.

By Joe Brentwood.

Say, have you seen my Harry, my little volunteer?
   As fine a lad as ever lived upon the Tennessee;
His voice so rich and cheery, his eye so bright and clear—
   Why has my darling ne'er come back to me?

He went to strike for freedom—to defend his State and
        home—
    When but sixteen at birth of May.
None looked so gay and bold, in garb of gray and gold;
    But I never saw him after they marched away.

*   *   *   *   *   *   *

The whippoorwill is calling to her mate upon the hill,
    As they did the night he went away;
And my heart is just as lonely, and the sorrow rankles
        still,
    When I sit alone and listen to the mournful, heartsick
        lay.

Oh, I reach my arms in yearning as I gaze towards the
        town,
    For he said he'd soon return to me;   ·
But my heart is broke with longing—he is so long in
        coming
    To the dear ones waiting here upon the Tennessee.

NEAR Allatoona, Ga., near what is known as
the Allatoona Pass, is a lone grave of an unknown
soldier, which is of considerable interest to
people along the Western and Atlantic Railroad,
through that region of battlefield, and which is
protected and cared for as sacred by the train
men whenever their duty brings them in that
vicinity. As you approach the northwestern
end of the Pass, immediately on the west side
of the track may be found this solitary grave.

At the head of the mound is a marble slab inscribed thus:

AN UNKNOWN HERO.
He Died for the Cause He Thought Was Right.
Here Rests the Precious Son of One of the Many Mothers
Whose Darling "Went Forth Never
to Return."

But whose son he was, and who watched for his return, only to be doomed to disappointment, is a question that will probably remain untold throughout eternity. Another question that arises in the mind of one who looks upon this lone grave is, Why should he, an unknown person, be cared for in this peculiar manner while hundreds of his comrades who fell on the same battlefield were thrown beneath the sod in a speedy manner, with never a stone to mark their resting places? This spot is also rendered historical by being the scene upon which the facts concerning and which inspired the famous gospel hymn, "Hold the Fort, for I Am Coming" were enacted.

REGINALD ROLAND.

GRAVE OF A GEORGIA VOLUNTEER.

IN a secluded vale a mile from Stribling sleeps in eternal repose one of that gallant Twelfth Georgia Regiment, commanded by Colonel, afterwards that brave Major-General, Edward Johnston. The hand of piety and patriotism neglected to remove the remains, with others of the heroic dead, to Staunton. In an excursion with a large party of ladies and gentlemen, the grave was discovered by "Zariffa" (Mrs. Marry Ashley Townsend, of New Orleans), whose charming, piquant pen has so often illuminated the sunny Southern hearth with "Thoughts that Breathe." Above this lonely grave her gifted pen, impromptu, sketched these beautiful lines, which will find a thrill in every Southern heart:

A GEORGIA VOLUNTEER.

Far up the lonely mountain side
  My wandering footsteps led,
The moss lay thick beneath my feet,
  The pine sighed overhead;
The trace of a dismantled fort
  Lay in the forest nave,
And in the shadow near my path
  I saw a soldier's grave.

The bramble wrestled with the weed
  Upon the lonely mound,
The simple head-board, rudely writ,
  Had rotted to the ground;
I raised it with a reverent hand,
  From dust its words to clear,
But time had blotted all but these:
  "A Georgia Volunteer."

I saw the toad and scaly snake
  From tangled coverts start,
And hide themselves amongst the weeds
  Above the dead man's heart;
But undisturbed in sleep profound,
  Unheeding, there he lay,
His coffin but the mountain soil,
  His shroud Confederate gray.

I heard the Shenandoah roll
  Along the vale below,
I saw the Alleghanies rise
  Towards the realms of snow;
The "Valley Campaign" rose to mind,
  Its leader's name—and then
I knew the sleeper had been one
  Of Stonewall Jackson's men.

Yet whence he came, what lip shall say?
  What tongue will ever tell
What desolated hearths and hearts
  Have been because he fell?
What sad eyed maiden braids her hair—
  Her hair which he held dear,
One lock of which perchance lies with
  The "Georgia Volunteer?"

What mother, with long watching eyes,
  And white lips cold and dumb,
Waits with appalling patience for
  Her darling boy to come?
Her boy! whose mountain grave swell up
  But one of many a scar
Cut on the face of our fair land
  By gory handed war.

What fights he fought, what wounds he wore,
    And all unknown to fame—
Remember, on his lonely grave
    There is not e'en a name;
That he fought well and bravely, too,
    And held his country dear,
We know, else he had never been
    "A Georgia Volunteer."

He sleeps; what need to question now
    If he were wrong or right?
He knows, ere this, whose cause was just
    In God the Father's sight;
He wields no warlike weapons now,
    Returns no foeman's thrust—
Who but a coward would revile
    An honest soldier's dust?

Roll Shenandoah, proudly roll
    Adown thy rocky glen,
Above thee lies the grave of one
    Of Stonewall Jackson's men!
Beneath the cedar and the pine,
    In solitude austere,
Unknown, unnamed, forgotten lies
    "A Georgia Volunteer."

THE VIRGINIA CADETS.

BATTLE of New Market, Virginia, in the Shenandoah Valley, May 15, 1864, in which 225 cadets of the Virginia Military Institute, of Lexington, Virginia, all between sixteen and

eighteen years old, acting as infantry, fought
on the Confederate side, capturing a Federal
battery after a gallant charge in which nine of
them were killed and forty-six wounded.

'Tion! dress! shoulder arms!
   Fours right! forward march!
That was how they kept us at it,
   Heads up stiff as starch.
We were Virginia boys—three hundred,
   In Virginia military school.
The war was raging North and South,
   And how could we fiery lads keep cool?

For we were bred in a battling time,
And our's was our father's creed—
The Old Dominion
In our opinion
Was bound for the South to bleed;
That being so, we'd all agree
That under the Lord and Robert Lee
The South was sure to succeed.

So every day it was " Shoulder arms!"
In a still battalion drill,
And every night there was news of a fight
With Lee in Richmond still;
While the men who stood
With gallant Hood
Held Tennessee with a royal will.

I reckon 'twas only good news we got
For we always gave it a cheer,
And when our three hundred loosed their lungs
'Twas something the deaf might hear.
To double up Grant was just the job,
We expected of Lee, and called him Bob,
Our brave old General Lee.

But it don't need bugles or rattling drums
To spread it around when bad news comes.
One day in May it was in the air
Like a ghost or a mist we felt it rise—
A droop to the lip
Of Colonel Ship.
A mournful flap to the company's flags,
A husky note to the Chaplain's prayer,
A cavalry Major dressed in rags
With gaunt, brown face, and with eager eyes
Clattering into the institute square.

"Virginia calls for her fighting sons."
That was all he he said, but its sharp appeal
Meant danger at hand from Federal guns—
A call to battle, and steel to steel.
Dumbly we stood for a moment's space
Then each lad lifted up his face,
On many a cheek a pitying tear,
But out from our hearts there rose a cheer,
And the Colonel, raising his hand, said then:
"I'll bring Virginia three hundred men!"

In a minute's time we were wild with joy
In all our ranks there was not a boy,
We had grown to be men at the Colonel's word.
The cavalry Major seemed in doubt:
"All under sixteen years old fall out!"
But never a lad from the company stirred,
If they'd wait the step of a single cadet
That young battalion would stand there yet.

Next morning though at the big bell's toll
We lacked twenty-five at muster roll.
"They are under the age," the Colonel said:
"Too young, God knows, for Yankee lead;"
To bring them to fight, the law forbids."

The Major said: " So we've caged the kids!"
But Lord how they cried with groans and tears
To be rated just once at sixteen years;
A'int seen the like since the war began,
And the smallest of all was the biggest man—
How he did beg and struggle and strive!"
Then we two hundred and seventy-five
Sent up a cheer for the little chap;
And the Captain of Company A
Saluting the Colonel, touched his cap,
And tossing his curly head did say:
"We'll fight for three hundred just the same."
Our flags here fluttered upon the wind.
We'll fight for Virginia, and all the South
Through storm and sunshine, fire and flame,
Up to the Yankee cannon's mouth.
God look to the men we leave behind. .
'Tion! dress! shoulder a'ms!

Rang out the loud command,
And we marched away
By noon that day
To fight for the Southern land;
Two-twenty-five with the infantry
And the rest with the guns in the battery,
Down by Shenandoh's grass banks.
And not a moustache in our marching ranks.

Next day we fell in with the conscripts rough
From the up-land farms with any sort of arms.
Day after that with the vet'rans tough
In their joy and their rags,
With their tattered flags;
And how they cheered us and made us proud,
As boldly we marched into camp and " allowed "
We were "jest sot up as men should be—
Fit for to fight under Old Bob Lee."

"Sigel is coming!" the word was spread,
"Pushing for Lynchburg straight ahead."
So the batteries limbered, the cavalry clanked;
Fires were put out, the infantry ranked,
And Breckinridge, grim as an iron man,
Rode off with his staff, and our fight began
Where the hills to the valleys roll gently down
And the pike runs by New Market Town.
Woods on the right, and a deep ravine
'Cross center and left lay there between
The boys in blue and the boys in gray.
In their battle rally
The batteries loudly beginning the fray
And a rain-storm driving up the valley.

The tale of the battle I cannot tell;
We stood 'till arose on our left the yell
Of the Southern boys, at the word "Advance!"
Then forward, too, with our hearts wild beating
And every throat the yell repeating.
"Capture the guns beyond the ravine!"
"Zip!" went the bullets past heedless ears;
"Chunk!" fell the shell, up rose our cheers,
Down the ravine with a rush and tumble,
Up the ravine with a pitch and stumble,
Out on the plateau. "Halt, form line!"
"On, double quick!" Crash came shell
Into our faces fired pell-mell;
A spurt of blood as the next boy fell;
Not mine? We were hit but never broke,
And charged like mad for the cannon smoke
With red quick flashes leaping from its heart,
Three hundred yards to the mouths of the guns.
"Virginia calls for her fighting sons!"
Here we are coming, as fall three score
In their blood and their pride;
And we rush below

Like a breaking tide,
Virginia boys!   Virginia's sons!
And—*we take the guns!*
Over the dead see our school flag float,
But our pride stops top of its mad joy, when
We hear from our General's rough old throat,
" Well done, Virginians!   Well done, *Men!*"

" I'M CONSCRIPTED, SMITH, CONSCRIPTED."

I'm conscripted, Smith, conscripted—
    Ebbs the subterfuges past,
And the sub-enrolling marshals
    Gather with the evening blast—
Let thine arms, oh! Smith support me,
    Hush your gab and close your ear,
Conscript-grabbers close upon you,
    Hunting for you far and near.

Though my scarred rheumatic " trotters "
    Bear me limping short no more;
And my shattered constitution
    Won't exempt me as before;
Though the provost guard surround me,
    Prompt to do their master's will,
I must to the front to perish—
    Die the great conscripted still.

Let not the seizer's servile minions
    Mock the lion thus laid low—
'Twas no fancy drink that " slewed " him—
    Whisky straight-out struck the blow.
I'm conscripted, Smith conscripted—
    Hark, you hear that grabber's cry;
Run, old Smith, my boy, they'll catch you,
    Take you to the front to die.

Sheridan's Raid in the James River Valley.

Prof. W. D. Cabell, Norwood Institute, Wash-
inton, D. C.

THE writer was attempting to burn the bridge
across the Tye River, where it empties into the
James, to impede Sheridan's progress, but found it
necessary to rip up the plank for ten or twenty
feet. I threw the flooring into the river when the
cavalry of Sheridan appeared in force, pursuing
my brother, Robert Stuart Cabell, and Ivanhoe
Cabell. To save their lives, I met them on the
bridge and turned them back into the lines of
the assembled cavalry. My brother had lost a
leg by a solid cannon ball at Fredericksburg.
and was unable to make his way on foot. They
obeyed my command, but, instead of surrender-
ing, rode through the lines of the United States
troops and made good their escape, after a five-
mile race, in open sight. with Spencer rifles
leveled and fired incessantly at them. The following lines, signed "Virginia," were written
by the authoress, Miss M. G. McClelland, whose
beautiful home, Elm Cottage, overlooked the
scene of the remarkable ride:

Down through the heart of our beautiful land
Swiftly and silently rode a strong band
Of Federal cavalry, spreading around

And behind them the piteous sound
Of destruction and burning and miserable pain,
Till even the echoes take up the refrain,
And all the bright, beautiful valley of James
Is blackened and ravaged with fury and flames.

Onward they come, relentless and strong,
Remorseless as fate, for to them shall belong
That cruelest, bitterest task in all war—
The bringing it home to the hearthstone and door,
The giving of homestead and barn to the torch,
The anguish of women and children for such
An end fate decrees shall always attend
Brother's strife against brother, friend against friend.

Swiftly and silent, remorseless and strong,
The dark blue thunder cloud rolls along,
Till the shades of evening begin to fall
Gently and calmly upon them all,
Victor and vanquished, friend and foe,
While the river murmurs in rythmic flow,
And the breezes bring from the mystic hill
God's own benison—"Peace, be still."

"Halt!" the order runs down the line.
What sound is borne on the sleepy wind?
Nearer and nearer, distant and clear,
The tramping of horses comes to the ear,
And down a road to the left of their course
Quickly there comes a galloping horse,
Then another, till, seeing the hostile train,
They turn and gallop the way they came.

Riding for life, while fuller and clearer
The sound of pursuit comes nearer and nearer.
Onward they dash in their desperate course,
Each man's life lies in the strength of his horse.
As they madly press on they well represent
The poor Southern Cause so broken and spent.

A boy in his teens, a man war-worn and lame,
While fierce on their track a regiment came.

"Keep near," groaned the man, with lips white and set;
"If I just keep the saddle we'll distance them yet.
Your hand quick, an instant—I am slipping, you see;
Oh, God! if that shell had but left me my knee
I'd still ride with the best.   Hark! they gain on us fast.
I'd give life for a pistol, to have but one last
Good shot at the blue coats, if just to requite
For the loss of my leg and this miserable flight.

"Don't turn your head," the boy eagerly cried;
"Speak not a word—for your life you must ride;
Down, flat on your horse, I'll guide him all right!
Put your arms 'round his neck—quick, the leader's in
		sight.
How you reel in your saddle; don't try to look 'round.
Ho! steady, good horse—my God, he is down!
We are in for it now; they have us both fast.
I said I'd stand by him, and I will to the last."

As a wild yell of triumph rings out on the air,
He springs from his horse with the strength of despair,
Grasps the man in his arms, lifts him on to his steed,
Leaps back on his own and puts both to its speed,
But turns in his saddle to give a loud shout
Of mocking defiance.   'Tis vain to call out
"Halt, or we fire!"   As well to command
The outgoing tide to return to the strand.

"Stop, men," cried the officer; "not a step more!
So gallant an action I never before
Beheld in a lad of his years.   Let them go.
To continue pursuit would serve but to show
Ourselves to be caitiffs unworthy the name
Both of soldiers and men.   I could hardly refrain
From cheering that brave 'little Reb' on the spot;
We'll return to the main body—forward, then, trot!"

'Tis many long years since the demon of war
Fled from our land. The grass grows o'er
Our ruins and graves. Still, when memory turns
To review our dead past, then deeds like this, boys,
Come to our remembrance and bid us rejoice
That, tho' ruined and conquered, we're still not undone
While our noble dead heroes yet live in their sons.

—VIRGINIA.

ANNIVERSARY OF APPOMATTOX.

STORY OF THE LAST SEVEN DAYS—EVACUATION OF RICHMOND AND THE RETREAT OF LEE.

Although what was in reality the final tragedy of the great civil war occurred at Appomattox on the 9th, when Lee's veterans, weary, footsore and starving, laid down their arms, the death warrant of the Confederacy was contained in the telegram from General Lee to President Davis, which was handed the latter in St. Paul's Church, in Richmond, on April 2d, 1865. Mrs. Sallie A. Putnam, in her "Richmond During the War," vividly describes the evacuation scenes and the feelings of those to whose hearts the Confederate cause was dear. After telling of the incident in St. Paul's Church, when President Davis received the telegram, she writes: "While these scenes were being enacted on the streets, indoors there was scarcely

less confusion and excitement. In every house
terror had penetrated. Ladies were busily engaged in collecting and selecting all the val-
uables possessed by them, together with cherished correspondence, yet they found time and
presence of mind to prepare a few comforts for
friends forced to depart with the Army of the
Government. Few tears. were shed; there was
no time for weakness and sentiment." Equally
vivid are Mrs. Putnam's description of the re-
lease of the convicts at the penitentiary and the
firing of the shops, the progress of the flames
in the city, the blowing up of the gunboats, the
explosion of the arsenal and magazines, etc.
"During the fire the Capitol Square," she says,
"presented a novel appearance. On the southeast and west of its lower half it was bounded
by burning buildings. The flames burst from
the windows, and rising from the roofs were
proclaiming in one wild roar their work of destruction. Myriads of sparks, borne upward by
the current of hot air, were brightening and
breaking in the dense smoke above. On the
sward of the square thousands of wretched crea-
tures, who had been driven from their dwellings
by the devouring flames, were huddled. But
here even it was almost as hot as a furnace.
The conflagration was the result of setting fire
to the tobacco warehouses and this step was

taken under a government order. Soon after
the capture of Savannah a law was passed by
the Confederate Congress requiring military
commanders to destroy articles of value rather
than allow them to fall into the hands of the
enemy. The dreadful tidings spread with the
swiftness of electricity from lip to lip; from
men, women and children the news was ban-
died, but many received it at first as only a
'Sunday sensation rumor.' Friend looked
into the face of friend to meet only an expression of incredulity, but later in the day as the
truth, stark and appalling, confronted us, the
answering look was that of stony, calm despair.
Late in the afternoon the signal of the evacuation became obvious even to the most incred-
ulous. Wagons were driven furiously through
the streets to the departments, where they received as freight the archives of the government
and carried them to the Danville depot to be
conveyed away by the railroad. Night came
on, but with it no sleep for human eyes in Richmond. Confusion worse confounded reigned
and grim terror spread in wild contagion. The
city council met and ordered the destruction of
all spirituous liquors, fearing in the excitement
there would be temptation to drink. In the
gutters ran a stream of whisky, and its fumes
impregnated the air. After nightfall Richmond

was ruled by a mob. In the principal section
of the city they surged in one black mass from
store to store, robbing them." Following the
evacuation of Richmond the events leading to
the surrender are quickly told, and in their telling the same grand spirit that has made the
Confederate soldier stand in history as unequaled for indomitable courage, devotion to
cause and superior prowess in arms, is shown to
have never deserted Lee's army, even to the
last moment, when the terms of surrender had
been fixed and orders to lay down their arms
had been given. Though it must have been
apparent to officer and private alike that the
cause was lost and further conflict would prove
futile, so far as perpetuating the Confederacy
was concerned, yet every man seemed to know
that each succeeding stand against the Federals
would increase or diminish the glory that would
be given to the Southern soldier in history. So,
apparently actuated solely by a desire and determination to emphasize their greatness as
soldiers, and make history in which the Southern posterity could eternally take pride, these
starving troops, the fragments of Lee's splendid
army that marched to Gettysburg, in each succeeding conflict during the seven days from
Petersburg to Appomattax battled with the same
esprit du corps that had given them victory

almost without exception when numbers were equal, and so often when the opposing forces were overwhelmingly in the majority. Five days passed without provisions being issued to the army. The end of the war was so apparent that every man in the ranks could note its approach, and it would be natural that an indifference and disorder would have marked the field work of the veterans in the closing days, but not so. Courage each time mounted with occasion, and Fitz Lee's cavalry met Sheridan's forces on the morning of April 9 and drove them before them, capturing two pieces of artillery, and manifesting the same military spirit that was shown by the Southern soldiers at Manassas, Antietam and Gettysburg. This declares them never to have been surpassed in devotion to cause, military discipline, response to command and determination to win battles.

On April 6th the rear guard was attacked by a large force of the enemy, and Generals G. W. C. Lee, Ewell and Anderson and many others were captured. General Rosser of the cavalry captured a body of 800 of the enemy, who had been sent by Grant under General Read to destroy the bridge at Farmville to impede Lee's march. On April the 7th Farmville was reached, and here for the first time since leaving Petersburg, April 2d, provisions were issued to the army. The enemy still pursuing, the quartermasters began to burn their wagons, and whatever they contained was destroyed. The enemy followed closely, crossed the railroad bridge, brought Lee to bay, attacked and were repulsed, and the retreat continued. On the evening of the 8th, with his army wearied, diminished in numbers by men falling by the wayside who had never before abandoned their colors, but were now unable to longer keep up with the retreating column, General Lee decided, after conference with his corps of officers, that he would advance the next day beyond Appomattox Courthouse, and if the force reported there should be only Sheridan's cavalry, disperse it and continue the march towards Lynchburg.

Gordon, whose corps had formed the rear guard from Petersburg, and who had fought daily for the trains, was now transferred to the front. Next morning; April 9, before daybreak, he, with Fitz Lee's cavalry moved forward to the attack. He was confronted by Sheridan's cavalry, and he drove them steadily before him and captured two pieces of artillery. All seemed going well when Sheridan withdrew from the field, and then, like the lifting of a curtain, Gordon beheld the army of the James advancing through the trees, with ten times his number. At the same time Longstreet, covering the rear, being threatened by Meade with a superior force, found it impossible to re-enforce Gordon, who, stained with powder and exhausted by his recent battle, reared his knightly head and said: "Tell General Lee my corps is reduced to a frazzle." Then it was that General Lee was forced to a conference with General Grant relative to surrender, and make the climax, and close the great American civil war drama which the world was watching. A flag of truce was accordingly raised to suspend hostilities pending the interview. An eye-witness thus describes General Lee's appearance when he rode off to see General Grant: "He was in full uniform, with handsome embroidered belt and dress sword, tall black army hat and buff leather gauntlets. His horse, old Traveler, was finely groomed, and his equipments, bridle, bit, etc., were polished until they shone like silver. He was accompanied by Colonel Marshall and Colonel Taylor, of his staff. Then followed the interview and the negotiations which fixed the terms of surrender. When General Lee rose to depart he went out upon the porch, and, after descending the steps, paused a moment and looked sadly out over the valley where his army lay, then mounted. General Grant, who had followed, * * * raised his hat in respectful salutation, as did those who stood on the porch. Upon observing

I.—16

this courtesy, General Lee, removing his hat, bowed low upon his horse's neck and rode away." Colonel William Miller Owens, in "In Camp and Battle," says: "As soon as he was seen riding toward his army, whole lines of men rushed down toward the roadside and crowded around him to shake his hand. All tried to show him the veneration and esteem in which they held him. Filled with emotion, he essayed to speak, but could only say: 'Men, we have fought through the war together. I have done the best I could for you. My heart is too full to say more.' We all knew the pathos of those simple words, of that slight tremble in his voice, and it was no shame on our manhood that 'something on a soldier's cheek washed off the stain of powder;' that our tears answered to those of our grand old chieftain, and that we could only grasp the hand of 'Uncle Robert' and pray 'God help you, General.'" So was the surrender of Lee brought on. The other armies followed his action soon, and the Southern soldiers turned for the first time their backs to the enemy and started to their desolated homes, to resume civic life and repair the wide-spread damage that war had wrought. The South to-day is the evidence of how splendidly the Confederate soldiers have labored in her rebuilding.

LEE AT APPOMATTOX.

BY J. A. BOOTY, LOS ANGELES, CAL.

The last gun was fired, the last roll was called,
Half starved, half naked, grim, gaunt, unappalled,
Stained with blood and powder the old army stood—
" I have done, my brave soldiers, all things for your good."

Thus spake their great leader, deep grief on his face,
While a halo of glory illumined the place.
Some trailed their muskets, some sheathed their swords,
They had smiled at Grant's cannon, they wept at Lee's
     words.

And Grant was as courteous as the grand knights of old;
No glad shouts were uttered, no loud drums were rolled,
And the victors saluted those gaunt men in gray.
And the fire-winged tempest died slowly away.

     No need have we for Northern foe,
     Living or dead, above, below,
     We honor those who wore the gray
     And weave for them our last bouquet.

     We war's arbitrament accept,
       And foeman leave in peace to rest,
     But when their graves are decked and wept
       The North shall do it, and Northwest.

     Had I but one, or, even grant,
       I had ten thousand flowers to plant,
     I'd put them all on Dixie's graves,
       My comrades, and our Southern braves.

General Lee's Ovation.

"General Robert E. Lee once told me of an ovation he received that touched him more ihan any ovation made in his honor," said the venerable Judge White, of Virginia, to a *Post* man at the National. "Following closely on the surrender of the Southern army, the commander-in-chief of the Confederacy went to pass a season at the home of his particular friend, E. R. Cocke. After a few weeks of the most hospitable and elegant entertainment, General Lee was called to the presidency of the Washington and Lee University. Bidding his kind friends adieu, he started for Lexington on horseback and alone. He had gone some miles and was passing through a rather dreary stretch of country, when he espied a plain old countryman mounted on a sorry nag coming toward him. As they passed each other both bowed, as is the fashion when strangers meet in out-of-the-way places; but the old farmer in the homespun suit stared hard at the soldierly figure, as through not quite certain of recognition. He went his way a little further, then turning his horse around, cantered back and soon came up with the general again. "I beg pardon, sir; but is not this General Robert Lee?" "Yes; I am General Lee. Did I ever meet you before, my friend?" Then the old Confederate grasped the chieftain's hand, and, with tears streaming down his face, said: "General Lee, do you mind if I cheer you?" The general assured him that he did not mind, and there on that lonesome pine-bordered highway, with no one else in sight, the old rebel veteran, with swinging hat, lifted up his voice in three ringing rounds of hurrahs for the man that the Southland idolized.

A PLEASANT party were on an excursion on the Potomac, when a singer rendered "Jesus, Lover of My Soul," to the comfort of every auditor. After the singing he was interrogated by a fellow passenger who referred to the peculiar intonation of his voice. When it became the satisfactory conclusion of both parties that the singer gave that same song when a sentinel in the war, the gentleman said to him. "That song saved your life. I heard you singing, detected thereby where you were and had my gun well upon you when you began the lines:

> "Cover my defenseless head
> With the shadow of Thy wing,"

When I took down my gun. I couldn't pull the trigger then." The singer recalled the particular occasion, that he was much depressed

that night and started the song which revived
memories of home.

———

   " 'Tis the soldier's life
To have his balmy slumbers waked with strife."

———

Our Battle Flag.

By H. L. Blanchard, Pensacola, Fla.

Furl that flag—furl it gently,
   Touch sacredly its tattered shred;
Blackened and riddled it speaks silently,
   Drooping and sad, of our honored dead.

It speaks of men who fought so valiantly,
   Now dead and forgotten—heroes unknown,
Who carried this flag; oh! how bravely,
   Until death claimed them his own.

It speaks of the heroes still living
   Who grasped this flag e'er it fell
From the clutch of a comrade falling,
   Bleeding and dying from the enemy's shell.

It speaks of a moment when all seemed lost—
   From our ranks an unforgotten shout arose;
With maddened rush at any cost
   We wrenched our flag from the hand of foes.

It speaks of combats desperately fought
   From the dawn of the day till the fall of night,
When in darkness with solemn thought
   We prayed for souls that had taken flight.

It speaks of that pure and unequaled fame,
   And our hearts grow sad and proudest then
As it utters that loved and cherished name
   Of heroines true—our Southern women.

It speaks of that awful and bitter day
   Our hearts bowed down—broken assunder.
Unconquered we stood, standing at bay,
   When suddenly came the word, " Surrender!"

For then did Lee, our grand old Chieftain,
   Loving us well—he knew 'twas best
To bow to the will of God, not man·-
   Our struggle was o'er—history tells the rest.

Furl it, brave comrade—furl it with care,
   This dear old flag, for which we bled,
That the ravages of time may never wear
   This silent epitaph of a cause that is dead,

THE CONFEDERATE BATTLE FLAG.

KATE FIELD wrote: ·· Speaking of General Johnston, I am reminded of the explanation he once gave me of the origin of the Confederate battle flag: ·At the battle of Bull Run the ·· Stars and Bars" proved a failure because they were so much like the Union colors. Indeed, both armies mistook their enemies for friends, and *vice versa*. After the battle I resolved to discard this flag, and called for each regiment to procure its State colors. This they were unable to do, and I asked the army for new designs. Among those presented one by General Beauregard was chosen, and I altered this only in making it square instead of oblong. This flag was afterwards adopted by the Confederate armies generally. It was a Greek cross of blue, with white stars on the blue bars. This flag. by the way. was designed by Colonel Walton. of Louisiana. and presented to General Beauregard.''

That Silver Moon Banner.

Dr. J. S. Carothers, Shannon, Miss.

We repeatedly heard during the war that among the many designs submitted to the War Department for battle flags, this one, the full-orbed silver moon in a blue field, surrounded by a white border, was designed by Brigadier General W. J. Hardee, who organized and commanded the troops afterwards commanded by Major General S. B. Buckner. and better known at the close of the war as Cleburne's Division, and that it was by him adopted as the ensign of his chivalrous troops, this right being a special grant by the authorities at Richmond for his division only. Cleburne's and Cheatham's divisions were the *Eng* and *Cheng*, Siamese twins of this Army of Tennessee. I remember the devices used on the retrograde movement in Georgia by the officers in these two commands, to control the men and disabuse their minds of the demoralization of a retreat. They would come quietly down the trenches at night, arouse the men and tell them we were going to relieve "Mars Frank's" boys, who had been roughly handled, probably repulsed, and our place would be filled by other troops. General Cheatham's boys were told that they were to go to retake works we had been driven from, etc., and we would not learn the true facts until a new line, or complete swapping of our flanks to checkmate a flank movement, was effected. Doubtless "Mars Frank's" boys, who marched under the cross of St. Andrew, and Pat's boys, under the full silver moon, will recall these ruses.

THE BUGLE CALL.

COLONEL JOHN MILLEDGE, OF GEORGIA.

I love to feel on my bridle-bit
　The champ of a thorough-bred,
When the bugle call and ringing hoof
　Tell of a charge ahead.

There is no sound, there is no song
  That stirs a soldier's soul
Like the bugle call and ringing hoof—
  In the charge of his brigade.

Refrain:

>   There is no sound, there is no song,
>   That stirs a soldier's soul,
>   Like the bugle call and ringing hoof
>   In the charge of his brigade.

In squadron front with closed ranks
  Together side by side,
With bounding steed and sabre raised
  Straight to the front we ride.
There is no fear, there is no doubt,
  But every man responds
To the bugle call and the ringing hoof
  In charge of his brigade.

When the battle's o'er, and the roll is called
  As in the ranks we stand,
There's many a horse that finds his place
  Without a guiding hand.
His rider 's gone and all alone
  He rushes to respond
To the bugle call and the ringing hoof
  In the charge of his brigade.

There's many a horse and many a man
  Who charging in the fray,
Together fight, together fall,
  Together pass away.
In years to come the mem'ry of these scenes
  Will still remain
Of the bugle call and the ringing hoof
  In charge of our brigade.

MEMORIES.

BY MRS. W. H. WILLIS.

Never was step more steady as the "band-box soldiers"
    filed
Out from the famed "Camp Jackson," while the gods
    looked down and smiled
On troops so fair and graceful in their stainless garb of
    gray;
Each man ready—each man panting—for the thickest of
    the fray.

They were leaving there in Portsmouth, in the city of her
    dead,
The first brave Georgia soldier who had bowed his gallant
    head
On the soil of old Virginia, pillowed on a spot so fair,
Where many a woman's tears had fallen above his golden
    hair.

He had yielded, ere the battle came, to "power none dare
    defy,"
And in a stranger land, poor boy, had lain him down to
    die;
But he was sweetly sleeping, in a calm, untroubled rest,
While fair hands strewed earth's loveliest flowers above
    his quiet breast.

And his comrades all were hasting to a fierce, baptismal
    fire—
Not a laggard in the ranks, from sturdy boy to gray-
    haired sire;
Each with a picture in his heart of a dear Southern home—
O, heaven, guard the homes till these brave wanderers
    come.

       *   *   *   *   *   *

How they "illustrated Georgia" all along the well-fought
  front,
As, 'mid the thickest of the fight, they bore the battle's
  brunt.
How proudly waved the Southern Cross where'er their lot
  was cast.
Ah, Hill, the "band-box soldiers" are the fighting force at
  last!

The patrician was the private, high of soul and pure of
  blood,
As if in armor clad, lo! how invincible he stood!
And on the weary road anon, a soldier without peer,
He marched along with bleeding feet and sang a song of
  cheer.

Many moons had waned and waned, yet they on either
  side
Of the classic old Potomac sternly fought and bravely died.
Grim death had aimed his cruel shaft at many a shining
  mark,
And had crossed the Stygian river with his overladen
  barque.
Tongue of mortal ne'er can tell it, history can never show
Half the valor of the Southron as he met his Northern foe.
While nations gazed, awe-stricken, on the bitter, un-
  matched fray,
Marveling the while they looked upon the troops who wore
  the gray.

O, grand old uniform of gray, so faded, worn and old,
Ye covered many a princely form and many a heart of
  gold.
What if they wore the rough old jeans in the dark hour of
  need?
"A man's a man for a' that," and these be men indeed.

On the fatal field, Cold Harbor, there, their gallant leader
    fell,
And strong men looked their last upon the form they loved
    so well,
While pale lips whispered to sad hearts so full of grief and
    pride,
"He had lived long enough, who in his country's cause
    had died."

Died at his post!   O, record meet for such exalted souls!
Who shall a fitter tribute as for our beloved Doles?
His life was o'er—mysterious fate denied him victory,
But blessed him at the last with glorious immortality.

Let us raise a fair white tablet o'er our honored Chieftain's
    breast
That shall tell in living words of him so early crowned and
    blest—
Of deathless love and memory, fresh from our hearts
    aglow,
And reverent passers-by shall say, "Behold! they loved
    him so!"

There is no love like this—it fills his soldier's heart to-day,
Its height and depth be measured not, it fadeth not away;
'Twas born upon the battlefield where brave men's souls
    were tried,
It burns in every warrior's breast whatever fate betide.

And sweet shall be his slumber in his own fair sunny clime,
For he sleeps in dear old Georgia, where for all the coming
    time
His flashing sword is sheathed, and with its warrior is laid
    down,
And the laurel wreath is but exchanged for the immortal
    crown.

General Hood's Last Charge.

By Mary Hunt McCaleb.

(General Hood left his orphan children to the care and
protection of his old Texas brigade.)

The twilight of death is beginning to fall,
Death's shadows are creeping high up on the wall,
  Eternity's waters are plashing
So close I can hear the wild waves as they roar
And sullenly break on the surf-beaten shore,
  Their silver spray over me dashing.

The old camp is fading away from my view,
I hear the last stroke of life's beating tattoo,
  The sound wears the muffle of sorrow,
My campaigns are ended, my battles are o'er,
My heroes will follow my lead nevermore,
  No roll call shall break on the morrow.

But now I am fighting them over again—
On fields that are gory 'mid heaps of the slain,
  The enemy swiftly are flying.
The shrieking of shell and the cannon's deep boom
Are thundering still at the gate of the tomb,
  The rattle of grape shot replying.

But ah! the last enemy conquers to-night,
And Death is the victor, and vain is the fight
  When God and his creature have striven;
The struggle is o'er life's colors are furled,
Are lost in the dark of the vanishing world,
  The bonds of the spirit are riven.

But ere I go down neath the conquerer's tread,
And lie white and still in the ranks of the dead
  Through silence forever unbroken,
To you, my old heroes, my Texas brigade,
From the dimness of death, from the cold of its shade,
  One last solemn charge must be spoken.

My faithful old followers, steady and true,
My children are orphans; I give them to you,
  A trust for your sacredest keeping;
By the shades of the heroes who fought by your side,
By the few who have lived, the many who died,
  By the brave army silently sleeping,

By the charges I lead where you followed so true,
When the soldiers in gray and the soldiers in blue
  And the blood of the bravest was flowing,
Be true to this last and this holiest trust,
Though the heart of your leader has crumbled to dust,
  And grasses above him are growing.

FROM HON. WASHINGTON GARDNER, OF MICHIGAN.

FRANKLIN, from the Confederate standpoint, must ever remain one of the saddest tragedies of the civil war. On the other hand, there were in that battle, possibilities to the Confederate cause that came near being realized, scarcely second to another in the great conflict. Had Hood won—and he came within an ace of it— and reaped the legitimate fruits of his victory, the verdict of history would have been reversed, and William Tecumseh Sherman, who took the flower of his army and with it made an unobstructed march to the sea, leaving but a remnant to contend against a foe that had taxed his every resource from Chattanooga to Atlanta, would have been called at the close, as at the beginning of the war, "Crazy Sherman." No individual—not even Hood himself—had so much at stake in the fight at Franklin as the hero of "the march to the sea."

MISSING.

In the cool, sweet hush of a wooded nook,
    Where the May buds sprinkle the green old sward,
And the winds and the birds and the limpid brook
    Murmur their dreams with a drowsy sound,
Who lies so stilly in the plushy moss,
    With his pale cheek pressed on a breezy pillow,
Couched where the light and the shadows cross
    Thro' the flickering fringe of the willow?
            Who lies, alas!
        So still, so chill, in the whispering grass?

A soldier clad in the zouave dress—
    A bright-haired man with his lips apart—
One hand thrown up o'er his frank, dead face,
    And the other clutching his pulseless heart,
Lies there in the shadow, cool and dim,
    His musket swept by a trailing bough,
With a careless grace on his quiet limbs
    And a wound on his manly brow.
            A wound, alas!
        Whence the warm blood dripped on the quiet grass.

The violets peer from their dusky beds,
  With a tearful dew in their great pure eyes;
The lilies quiver their shining heads,
  Their pale lips full of sad surprise,
And the lizzard darts through the glistening fern,
  And the squirrel rustles the branches hoary,
Strange birds fly out with a cry to bathe
  Their wings in the sun-set glory.
            While the shadows pass
      O'er the quiet face, and dewy grass.

God pity the bride who waits at home
  With her lily cheeks and her violet eyes,
Dreaming the sweet old dreams of love,
  While her lover is walking in Paradise.
God strengthen her heart as the days go by,
  And the long dreary nights of her vigil follow—
No bird, no moon, nor whispering wind
  May breathe the tale of the hollow;
            Alas!   Alas!
      The secret is safe with the woodland grass.

The above lines were written after the battle of Seven
Pines, suggested by the report of the missing.

The following beautiful verses on the death
of Zollicoffer, were written by Harry Flash, of
Mobile, while a voluntary aid of General
Hardee:

      First in the fight and first in the arms
        Of white-winged angels of glory,
      With the heart of the South at the feet of God
        And his wounds to tell the story.

The blood which flowed from his hero heart
  On the spot where he nobly perished,
Was drank by the earth as a sacrament
  In the holy cause he cherished.

In heaven a home, with the brave and blest,
  And for his soul's sustaining,
The Apocalyptic eyes of Christ
  And nothing on earth remaining

But a handful of dust in the land of his choice,
  A name in song and story;
And fame to shout with her trumpet voice,
  Died on the field of glory!

LONGSTREET ON THE WAR.

THE Government, moved, doubtless, by a desire
to protect our soil as much as possible, kept our
troops scattered and thus made them inefficient.
There was scarcely a time when we had a really
grand army at any one point. The policy of
the Federals and especially Gen. Grant's policy,
was to mass everything available at one point
and then drive straight at it. Of course our
government disliked to leave any section of the
Confederacy at the mercy of the Federals.
Therefore our men were scattered over our
whole extent of territory. I do not think that
our best generals even comprehended the necessity of concentrating of forces. They relied too

much on the valor of their men. They seemed to forget that where good cautious generals commanded on each side numbers must triumph over valor. There was a notable instance of this at Fort Donelson. Gen. Albert Sidney Johnston, one of the loftiest souls that ever lived, had about 45,000 men. Of this force 15,000 were at Donelson, 15,000 at Columbus and 15,000 in front of Buell. Grant having a force of about 30,000 men fell upon Donelson and captured it. Had Johnston ever concentrated his forces at Donelson or in front of Buell he could have crushed either Grant or Buell. As it was, General Grant told me afterwards that he was as badly whipped at Donelson as the Confederates were if the Confederates had only known it and been able to act upon their knowledge. I am inclined to think that General Joe Johnston was the ablest and most accomplished man that the Confederate armies produced. He never had the opportunity accorded to many others, but he showed the wonderful power as a tactician and a commander. I do not think we had his equal for handling an army and conducting a campaign.

Gen Lee was a great leader—wise, deep and sagacious. His moral influence was something wonderful. But he lost his praise on certain occasions. No one who is acquainted with the fact could have believed that he would have fought the battle of Gettysburg had he not been under great excitement, or that he would have ordered the sacrifice of Pickett and his Virginians on the day after the battle. He said to me afterward, ''Why didn't you stop all that thing that day?'' At the Wilderness when our lines had been driven in and I was just getting to the field, Gen. Lee put himself at the head of one of my brigades, and leading it into action my men pressed him back, and I said to him that if he would leave my command in my own hands I would re-form his lines. His great soul rose masterful within him when a crisis or disorder threatened. I loved Gen. Lee as a brother while he lived, and I revere his memory. He was a great man, a born leader, a wise general, but I think Johnston was the most accomplished and capable leader that we had. Grant was incomparably the greatest general on the Northern side. He possessed an individuality that impressed itself upon all that he did.

McClellan was a skillful engineer, but never rose above the average conclusions of his council. Sherman never fought a great battle, and displayed no extraordinary power. But Grant was great. He understood the terrible power of concentration and persistency. How stubbornly he stuck to Vicksburg and to Richmond. He concentrated all his strength, trained his energies to a single purpose, and then delivered terrible sledge-hammer blows, against which strategy. tactics and valor could avail nothing. He knew that majorities if properly handled must triumph in war as in politics, and he always gathered his resources together before striking.

Gettysburg was the most desperate battle of the war. There was never any fighting done anywhere to surpass the battle made by my men on the 2d of July. I led 12,000 men into that charge. Over one-third of this number were killed or wounded. These veterans charged the whole Federal army, intrenched on a crest. harassed on each flank until the line was stretched, and at last I found myself charging 50.000 intrenched men in face of a volcano of artillery with a single line of battle. My two divisions encountered and drove back the Third Corps, the Fifth Corps, the Sixth Corps, the Second Corps, one of the divisions of the Twelfth and the Pennsylvania Reserves. As they broke line after line they encountered new ones and felt the steady shock of fresh troops. The Federals contend that the bulk of Lee's army was in this charge, and put the strength of the attacking column at 45.000 men, when it was only my 12,000 with 2,000 of these knocked out of ranks before they had hardly started up the slope. I do not think the records of the war can show anything to approach this work. I agreed with Lee as to necessity of surrender at Appomattox. For some time I had felt we were fighting against hope. I kept my lips closed and fought ahead in silence. For the week preceding the surrender I fought almost without ceasing. I was covering General Lee's retreat while Gordon opened a way for him in front. I had Fields Division, all that was left. The Federals pressed upon us relentlessly, and we fell back fighting night and day, inch by inch, covering the slow 'retreat of our wagon trains. Our lines were never once broken or disordered. My men fought with the finest regularity and heroism. Wherever I placed a brigade there it would stand until I ordered it away. I was among my men constantly, so that I knew little of the great situation. Early in the morning General Lee sent for me, and I at once went to him. He was in deep concern. He stated to me that his retreat had been cut off and it was impossible for him to escape from the circle that had been drawn about him. "In that case, General," I replied, "you should surrender the army. If escape is impossible, not another life should be sacrificed." General Lee then began to talk about the distress and trouble that a surrender would bring upon the country and his people. "That cannot be put against the useless shedding of these brave men's blood. The people will know that you have done all that man can do." He then told me he had discovered there were heavy masses of infantry in front and that he could not hope to cut through. It was a terrible moment for General Lee. Having fought for years with high and lofty purposes, having won victory after victory and made a record for his army not equalled in history, it was hard that he must surrender everything.

ALBERT SIDNEY JOHNSTON.

Honor to him who only drew
  In Freedom's cause his battle blade
And 'round our Southern banners threw
  A halo that can never fade.
Honor to him whose name sublime
  Shall be the watchword of the free;
When yet the latest wave of time
  Shall break on far eternity.

In artless truth, a simple child;
  In valor, first of God-like men,
Who, tho' his countrymen reviled,
  Did ne'er revile again.
Like some lone rock, 'gainst which the flow
  Of fickle passions foam and fret.
Unmoved, our dear dead captain stood,
  Firm planted in his purpose yet.

What, though detraction grieved the heart
  That bled but for his country's woe,
He recked not, but of his country's part
  To shield her weakness from the foe.
He gave his bosom to the storm
  That rose in curses on the air,
Courting the shafts that might not harm
  His country while they rankled there.

Slow falling back from Bowling Green,
  His crippled columns move along,
While, flanking every side, were seen
  The myriad hosts of human wrong,
Curtained beneath his clear, calm eye,
  The heroic impulse held its sway,
Till, turning in his path to die,
  The wounded lion stands at bay.

Ah! how he stood and where he stood,
  Where strong men perished in their strength,
On Shiloh's field of death and blood
  His bolted thunders fell at length.
The fires of vengeance, hot and red,
  Far flashed where rode his knightly form,
And wreck and rout and ruin spread
  Where swept that day his battle storm.

Oh, peace to him who slumbers now
  Beneath the soil he died to save.
The wreath that decks his clay cold brow
  Shall blossom in the martyr's grave;
Shall blossom where in after time
  Our children's children bless the mold
Where Sidney Johnston sleeps sublime,
  Like some great mastodon of old.

DEATH OF GENERAL LEONIDAS POLK

On the Kennesaw Mountain.

BY HENRY LINDEN FLASH.

A flash from the edge of the hostile trench,
  A puff of smoke, a roar,
Whose echo shall roll from the Kennesaw hill
  To the furthermost Christian shore.
Proclaim to the world that the warrior priest
  Will battle for right no more.

And that for a cause which is sanctified
  By the blood of martyrs unknown—
A cause for which they gave their lives,
  And for which he gave his own—
He kneels a meek embassador
  At the foot of the Father's throne.

And up to the courts of another world
  That angels alone have trod,
He lives away from the din and strife
  Of this blood-besprinkled sod—
Crowned with the amaranthine wreath
  That is worn by the blest of God!

HIGH TIDE AT GETTYSBURG.

WILL H. THOMPSON.

A cloud possessed the hollow field,
The gathering battle's smoky shield
Athwart the gloom the lightning flashed,
And through the cloud some horsemen dashed,
And from the heights the thunder pealed.

Then at the brief command of Lee
Moved out that matchless infantry,
With Pickett leading grandly down
To rush against the roaring crown
Of those dread heights of destiny.

Far heard above the angry guns,
A cry across the tumult runs,
The voice that rang through Shiloh's woods
And Chickamauga's solitudes,
The fierce South cheering on her sons.

Ah! how the withering tempest blew
Against the front of Pettigrew!
A khamsin wind that scorched and singed
Like that infernal flame that fringed
The British squares at Waterloo.

A thousand fell where Kemper led;
A thousand died where Garnett bled.
In blinding flame and strangling smoke,
The remnant through the batteries broke
And crossed the works with Armistead.

"Once more in Glory's van with me!"
Virginia cries to Tennessee:
"We two together, come what may,
Shall stand upon those works to-day,
The reddest day in history."

Brave Tennessee! Reckless the way!
Virginia heard her comrade say:
"Close round this rent and riddled rag,
What time she set her battle flag
Amid the guns of Doubleday."

But who shall break the guards that wait
Before the awful face of fate?
The tattered standards of the South
Were shriveled at the cannon's mouth,
And all her hopes were desolate.

In vain the Tennesseean set
His breast against the bayonet;
In vain Virginia charged and raged,
A tigress in her wrath encaged,
  'Till all the hill was red and wet.

Above the bayonets mixed and crossed
Men saw a gray, gigantic ghost
Receding through the battle cloud,
And heard across the tempet loud
  The death cry of a nation lost.

The brave went down; without disgrace
They leaped to Ruin's red embrace;
They only heard Fame's thunder wake,
And saw the dazzling sunburst break
  In smiles on Glory's bloody face.

They fell, who lifted up a hand
And bade the sun in heaven to stand;
They smote and fell, who smote the bars,
Against the progress of the stars
  And stayed the march of Motherland.

They stood, who saw the future come
On through the fight's delirium;
They smote and stood, who held the hope
Of nations on that slippery slope,
  Amid the cheers of Christendom.

God lives! He forged the iron will
That clutched and held the trembling hill;
God lives and reigns; He built and lent
The heights for Freedom's battlement,
  Where floats her flag in triumph still.

Fold up the banners! Smelt the guns!
Love rules. Her gentler purpose runs.
A mighty Mother turns in tears
The pages of her battle years,
  Lamenting all her fallen sons!

LAST DAYS OF THE ARMY OF TENNESSEE.
"HALT! Camp at full distance, unload your guns, stack them and rest at ease." At this all field officers seemed to retire into the thick woods that surrounded us to hide their faces for a time, and left us to draw full rations from our imaginations. We looked and listened in the death-like silence for an answer to our hungry thoughts. We saw our guns left without a guard; our cannon was left alone in open ground. No picket had been put out to herald the approach of our enemies, who had been following us for two days. We listened closely and expectantly for orders to build breastworks, but no orders came. We sat and dreamed. We walked around. What was happening in that once jubilant army? Now it was so still. Only the neigh of hungry horses broke the death-like stillness. In this awful silence and stupor the trees, the shadows seemed to sigh. "Death, Death." The stillness is broken as if by magic. The thunder tones of the enemy's cannon, familiar, oft-repeated, over hill and dale, and through the woodland on the right and on the left behind us. We rush to our posts and wait for orders to fall into line. We listen for the bugle and breathlessly wait for the long roll, but no bugle sounds, and no orders to fall in * * * We see the field officers and they ride slowly

about and seem to be dreaming. When one is asked to explain what this awful suspense means, he only answers, "I don't know; but something will be known to-night on dress parade." The suspense only increases as time passes until dress parade is called. Each eager to be first, a line is formed in less time than ever before. All are ready and eager to hear, yet afraid to hear. The adjutant walks out in front of the line, but he looks downcast. His walk, his features tell that unwelcome news or some evil forebodings await us. When he pulls from his pocket a piece of brown paper, he says: "Soldiers, this is hard to read; not because it is not well written, but because of what it contains." His voice is husky as he reads: "'Robt. E. Lee has surrendered, and we are now entering a ten days' armistice.' That's all. Officers, return your companies to their respective quarters."

Ah, yes! the cannon that have thundered all day in the rejoicing of the enemy! Will we also have to give up? If so, where will we be carried? What is the end? Will we go home to see the dear ones that we have not seen in so long? Will we ever know whether they are yet alive, or will we, must we, fill the prisons of the conquerors? "Yes;" "No;" is answered. In this strain we are left until the thunder tones of Lincoln's death resound from end to end of our army. Ten thousand men join Joe Wheeler to cut through the enemy and try to escape to Texas. But soon the order declared a hopeless undertaking is canceled. * * * We made out our muster rolls and drew our rations. Joe Johnston issued to us the $30,000 in silver that Jefferson Davis had given him for his services to the Confeceracy. We started home without even seeing the United States Army, with our colors floating in the breeze, not knowing yet that it was a conquered banner. Then as we did pass outside the enemy's line, our sad faces received sympathy from the "boys in blue," and bidding them all a comrade's farewell, we marched on homeward. But, oh, the heartaches on that march!   J. T. C.

General Custer's Tribute to the Conquered Foe.

Speaking of Custer's charge on the evening of the 6th of April, 1865, and its repulse, the closing of the Federal lines around the Confederates, and the last conflict at Sailor's Creek, a Union soldier states: "Every cloud has its silver lining. The next morning, after a refreshing slumber on the sweetest of all beds—the bare ground

—we were again marshaled in line, and down that line came General Custer, his yellow hair and boyish face well known to all of us. Near the center of the line, he turned to his band, and ordered it to play "Dixie." As the marvelous strains of that Confederate war song floated in liquid sweetness around us and over us, we broke into tumultuous cheering. General Custer waved his hat, and a thousand gallant soldiers in blue dashed caps in the air." Such was General Custer in the presence of a conquered foe. Here might the artist have found his inspiration for "Custer's Last Rally." and the Southern poet who wrote:

> The nations of the earth shall know
> That love, not hate, alone can glow
> In soldier hearts by valor tried,
> On many a field, and this our pride.

The immortal soul of Jefferson Davis passed from earth on Friday. December 6, 1889.

> "Davis is dead!" the message read,
>   The night was waning fast;
>   On lightning wings the sentence sped;
>   A storm of pent-up tears unshed
>   Came gushing forth at last.

"Davis is dead!" the message read.
  We thought of days gone by
And him whose dauntless courage fed
The altar fires when hope had fled,
  And darkness veiled the sky!

"Davis is dead!" the message read.
  God keep his noble name;
The deeds of those who fought and bled
For Dixie are eternal wed
  With his undying fame!

"Davis is dead!" the message read;
  Last of a princely train.
Though lowly lies his crownless head,
His memory lives, and in his stead
  No other king shall reign!

                MONTGOMERY M. FULSOM.

OUR DEAD CHIEF.

Come, brothers of our Southern land—
Members of that historic band
  Who gladly wore the gray—
Come, let us morn our fallen chief;
Let us in sackcloth and grief,
  In sorrow weep to-day.

A man of wondrous gifts is gone,
A man with kingly graces born,
  A warrior, statesman—dead.
"Our President," through bloody wars—
  A martyr to a glorious cause—
  For us his heart has bled.

He grandly lived a silent life
Since turning from all whirl and strife,
  And bore a breaking heart.
The target of a hundred pens,
Aflame with hate, their arrow sends
  Full many a poisoned dart.

There meets my gaze on yonder wall
A pictured group in public hall.
  In days when hearts were tried
A brilliant galaxy they be—
Hill, Jackson, Stuart, knightly Lee—
  Virginia's sons—her pride.

Our honored chief 's among the band.
He sits—the others round him stand,
  A nobler conclave never.
All have been called—yes, one by one—
Leaving the grand old man alone.
  Now, he has crossed the river.

Come, brothers; gather 'round his bier,
And touch it with the falling tear,
  Which wells from streaming eyes.
No fitter tribute can we bring
Than loyal hearts, and souls whence spring
  Love reaching to the skies.
—Mrs. J. William Jones.

In 1867 Bishop O. P. Fitzgerald, editor of the *Christian Spectator*, San Francisco, Cal., collected and remitted to the relief committee of the South over *ninety thousand* dollars for the suffering people. By special request one remittance was made directly to General Lee for the benefit of the families of deceased Confederate Virginia soldiers. The following reply was sent:

LEXINGTON, VA., June 1, 1867.

MY DEAR SIR—I received from Messrs. Lee & Waller, New York, $509.00 in gold forwarded by you for the widows and orphans of Southern soldiers in Virginia. I will endeavor to apply for the relief of those most requiring aid.

I hope you will permit me to express my individual thanks to you and the generous donors for the aid thus given the suffering women and children of Virginia, whose grateful prayers in your behalf will, I am sure, be registered in heaven. With great respect, your obedient servant, R. E. LEE.

Rev. O. P. Fitzgerald.

Californians should ever be remembered with gratitude for their great kindness during the period referred to. There was sent to Nashville $3,300 of this fund.

"STONEWALL" JACKSON.

He sleeps 'neath the soil that the hero loved well,
  In the land of his birth, his own Sunny South.
He hated oppression as millions can tell,
  Nor feared the grim king at the fierce cannon's mouth.

'Mid the brave he was bravest—the noblest of all,
  In virtue was peerless, a halo cf light
He shed o'er the land that now mourns the fall
  Of the chieftain, the hero, the valiant in fight.

He needs not a costly mausoleum nor urn
  To point out the spot where he sleeps in his grave,
For like living fire his virtues will burn,
  So long as earth honors the gallant and brave;
His name is a talisman shielding our land
  Which will guide the brave soldier to glory and fame.
The truest and bravest in our peerless land
  Will vie in great deeds at the sound of his name.

But never again 'mid the hoarse cannon's roar,
  Shall our brave boys hear "Stonewall" give earthly
      command;
He has fought the good fight, and on Canaan's bright shore
  He wears a rich crown cn the Savior's right hand.
The hero, the soldier has passed from our sight,
  'Mid the victorious sounds of a nation, whose joy
Is saddened to think that the peerless in might,
  Has fled to the mansions in yonder blue sky.
                                    —L. H. M.
Huntsville, Ala., May 18, 1863.

A Tribute To Jefferson Davis.

By Bettie Houston Littlepage.

Jefferson Davis! softly breathe
  The name so grandly worn
By one who each reverse of fate
  For years has nobly borne.

A leader on the battlefield,
  Of courage cool and high,
He led his men to victory
  Beneath a tropic sky.

A leader in the council hall,
  Our chosen one he stood,
On whom each Southern heart relied
  For counsel sage and good.

And when defeat had thrown a pall
  Of darkness o'er the land,
On him Oppression chose to lay
  A heavy, cruel hand.

They took each right a freeman claims,
  And sought to tear away
The wreath of love our Southland placed
  Upon his locks of gray.

But to our chief, in his retreat,
  Each loyal Southron turned,
And over his indignities
  Our pride so fiercely burned.

Each wound they gave to his proud heart
  A hundred thousand bore,
Who loved the Lost Cause tenderly,
  And the gray that Davis wore.

He was a martyr for our sakes,
  A king without a throne;
And Southern chivalry gave to him
  More than the world has known

Of homage, springing from the heart,
  A love so deep and strong,
A grand-voiced bard will yet arise
  To weave it into song.

But jealousy and hate may cease,
   For list! a funeral knell!
The flags are floating at half mast,
   And tolls the passing bell.

Each Southern heart is bowed with pain,
   And eyes are dim with tears;
We softly breathe the honored name
   Which memory so endears.

For, lying in a hall of state,
   Upon a flower-strewn bed,
A sorrowing people gather round
   Our chieftain, cold and dead.

But Fame will place upon its scroll
   His name that cannot die,
And proudly blazon it abroad
   As Time speeds swiftly by.

For prejudice will pass away,
   And History will give
The meed of praise, so justly due,
   And bid his memory live.

He needs no highly sculptured urn—
   No ode, nor funeral lay;
He'll live forever in the hearts
   Of all who love the gray.

TRIBUTE TO CAPT. EDWARD CROCKETT.

IN reviewing the past, and calling to mind some
of the heroes who crossed the silent river in defense of a cause though lost, yet sacred, still 1

think there is no one more worthy of notice than Capt. Edward Crockett, who quietly sleeps at Chickamauga. Having been a member of his company (A, thirteenth regiment) it was on the last day of the fight (Sunday) while at the head of his company, and sword aloft, that his star went down. There is no slab to mark his last resting place; yet each surviving member of old Company A, who followed him in this terrible onslaught, carries in memory's casket in letters of living gold, the name of Capt. Edward R. Crockett.

H. H. HOCKERSMITH.

Woodburn, Ky.

FURL THAT BANNER.

BY FATHER RYAN.

Take that banner down, 't is weary;
'Round its staff 't is drooping dreary;
　　Furl it, fold it, let it rest,
For there is not a man to wave it,
For there is not a sword to save it,
And its foes not scorn and brave it
In the blood that heroes gave it—
　　Furl it, hide it, let it rest.

Take that banner down, 't is tattered;
Broken is its staff, and shattered,
And the valiant hosts are scattered,
　　Over whom it floated high.
O, 't is hard for us to fold it;
Hard to think there's none to hold it;

Hard that those that unrolled it
   Now must furl it with a sigh.

Furl that banner, furl it sadly—
Once six millions hailed it gladly,
And ten thousand wildly, madly,
   Swore it should forever wave—
Swore that foeman's sword should never
Hearts, like theirs entwined, dissever,
And that flag should float forever
   O'er their freedom or their grave.

Furl it, for the hands that grasped it
And the hearts that fondly clasped it,
   Cold and dead are lying low;
And that banner, it is trailing,
While above it sounds the wailing
   Of its people in their woe,
For, though conquered, they adore it—
Love the cold dead hands that bore it—
Pardon those who trailed and tore it;
O, how wildly they deplore it
   Now to furl and fold it so.

Furl that banner, true 't is gory,
Yet 't is wreathed around with glory,
And 't will live in song and story
   Though its folds are in the dust;
For its fame, on brightest pages
Penned by poets and by sages.
Shall go sounding down the ages,
   Furl its folds though now we must.

Furl that banner softly, slowly,
Furl it gently; it is holy,
   For it droops above the dead.
Touch it not, unfurl it never,
Let it droop there furled forever,
   For its people's hopes are fled.

The Confederate Note.

By Major S. A. Jones, of Aberdeen, Miss.

Representing nothing on God's earth now,
  And naught in the waters below it;
As a pledge of a nation that's dead and gone,
  Keep it, dear friend, and show it.
Show it to those who will lend an ear
  To the tale that this paper can tell,
Of liberty born of the patriot's dream,
  Of a storm-cradled nation that fell.

Too poor to possess the precious ores,
  And too much of a stranger to borrow,
We issued to-day our promises to pay,
  Hoping to redeem on the morrow.
But days flew by, weeks became years,
  Our coffers were empty still,
Coin was so scarce our treasury'd quake
  If a dollar would drop in the till.

It looked in our eyes a promise to pay,
  And each patriot believed it.
We knew it had scarcely a value in gold,
  Yet as gold the soldiers received it,
But the faith that was in us was strong indeed,
  And our poverty well discerned,
And these little checks represented the pay
  That our suffering veterans earned.

But our boys thought little of prize or pay,
  Or of bills that were over due;
We knew if it brought us our bread to-day
  'Twas the best our poor country could do.
Keep it, it tells our history o'er,
  From the birth of the dream to its last.
Modest and born of the angel of hope,
  Like our hope of successs it passed.

Reply From Across "The Chasm."

Thanks, worthy friend, most heartfelt thanks,
  Both for the gift so kindly sent
And for the lesson by it taught
  Of wisdom and content.

Say not it represented naught,
  For to my mind its worth
This day exceeds the fondest hopes
  Of those who sent it forth.

What thoughts of dangers bravely met,
  Of hardships calmly borne,
Of hopes deferred and sickened hearts,
  Through winter and through storm.

Come to our minds while yet we gaze
  On "promises to pay,"
Which ne'er were paid and ne'er shall be
  Until the judgment day.

'Tis ever thus with this world's hopes,
  We plan and work and pray,
But God knows best and blesses us
  In his own time and way.

His way is best! Could we but feel
  How sure his blessings are,
Our promises would be far less,
  Our doings would be more.

Like foes we met on hostile fields,
  When this money bought you bread:
Like brothers now we meet again
  Since demon, war, has fled.

Warned by our sorrows in the past,
  May we like brothers stand
Shoulder to shoulder in resolve
  To guard our native land.

Invincible we then shall be,
  Armed with truth and right,
Ready to help each suffering soul
  That seeketh aid or light.

Then say not they are valueless,
  For the lessons they have taught
May be of value greater far
  Than could with gold be bought.

THE SOLDIER'S RETURN.

BY ANNA WARD.

Did he come in the pride of manhood,
  Flushed with a soldier's fame?
Did he hear a voice of welcome,
  A joy that breathed his name?
Did they meet the proud young brother,
  And kiss the bay-wreathed brow?
Did his presence in the homestead
  Bring the sunshine's olden glow?

Did the mother's heart beat happy,
  As she brushed away a tear—
While her heart spoke its thanksgiving,
  And silently its prayer?
Did the father's aged footsteps
  Hasten to meet his boy,
And bless the glowing sunlight
  Which brought such holy joy?

Ah, no! through hall and parlor,
  Sad footsteps echo now.
They bear a soldier's coffin,
  With measured steps and slow—

Back home, from whence he lately
  Answered his country's call.
They bear it over the threshold,
  The soldier's funeral pall.

No ray of a bright, glad welcome,
  But there entereth a dart
Which bringeth a cry of anguish,
  The wail of a broken heart—
The wail of a stricken mother,
  A sister's anguished moan,
A brother's heart-wrung sorrow,
  A father's tortured groan.

Out 'neath the clouded heaven,
  From the home he knew no more,
They bear the brave young brother
  Whose soldier's life is o'er.
Ne'er to the call of loved ones
He'll wake; they bear him lightly,
The dead to his narrow home.

The clod falls so hurtling
  O'er his coffined breast,
  Yet breaks not the soldier's rest.

Not a struggling sunbeam lingers
  O'er his coffined breast,
Yet breaks not the soldier's slumber,
  Or troubles his dreamless rest.
Not a struggling sunbeam lingers
  Over the red low grave;
The rain sweeps over the hill top
  A requiem to the brave.

Yet, mourners, there is Honor
  Shining o'er his grave,
A nation's tear its tribute,

Shed for the youngest brave;
And God bends down with healing
To grief so deep and fell,
He chasteneth with sorrow,
He doeth all things well.

January, 1862.

— —

GEN. E. KIRBY SMITH.

THE LAST LIVING GENERAL OF THE SOUTHERN WAR.

GENERAL E. Kirby Smith is today alone in that gloomy atmosphere of defeated, but proud and honored leadership in which walked and breathed the seven generals who headed the Lost Cause. One by one they have passed away into that land where there is no more of slavery, no more of war, no more of heartaches and despoiled hopes and ambitions. So that now General Kirby Smith stands alone on the shores of that limitless sea across which his fellow generals have passed away.

Robert E. Lee has gone. So has Samuel Cooper, once head of all. Gone, too, have Bragg, Albert Sidney and Joseph E. Johnston. And before a second sun shall have passed over the fields and forests of Southland the bones of Beauregard will have been borne away in state from beneath those same arches which have scarcely lost the echo of the mourning voices that were heard over the bier of Jefferson Davis. So that now of all that brilliant array of manhood and military genius the luster of whose achievements shone into the remotest parts of the earth but one remains—Gen. E. Kirby Smith.

He was wounded at the first battle of Manassas, a Minie ball passing through from one shoulder to the other. He was second in command to Johnston. Picture, if you can, an aged, white-haired man, lean and graceful; a man of fire, whose soul shining through his dark eyes seems to have been made but the warmer and brighter for the snows which cover his head and beard. The thick dark curls of his youth no longer cluster about his brow. The long beard, white as the driven snow, sweeping over his dark coat front first attracts the attention.

Trabling Back to Georgia.

By C. D. Blake.

I'se trabling back to Georgia,
Dat good, old land to see—
The place I left to wander
The day I was free.

I'se getting old and weary,
　And tired of roaming, too;
So, on my way to Dixie,
　I'll say good-bye to you.

CHORUS.

I'se trabling back—yes, trabling back;
　I'se trabling night and day.
I'se trabling back to Georgia,
　For I can not keep away.

I'se trabling back to Georgia,
　The place where I was born,
Among the fields of cotton,
　The sugar-cane and corn.
So happy with old massa,
　A living in the lane.
To see the old plantation,
　I'se trabling back again.
　　　　　[Chorus.]

To live and die in Georgia,
　Dats good enough for me.
I'll hoe de corn and cotton,
　And, oh, so happy be.
I'll hunt the coon and 'possum,
　And dance and sing and play;
And when I once get back there,
　I'll never come away.
　　　　　[Chorus.]

I'se trabling back to Georgia,
　To see the darkies there,
And see my old Aunt Dinah.
　Oh, golly, won't she stare.
We'll dance all night—till mornin'—
　By banjo's sweet refrain,
And have a celebration,
　When I get back again.
　　　　　[Chorus.]

The Pickett Charge.

From Members of the General's Staff at Gettysburg.

When the division arrived on the battle-field on that morning it took a position slightly in the rear of the artillery commanded by Colonel E. P. Alexander, and General Pickett was directed to hold himself in readiness to move against the enemy's position whenever notified by Colonel Alexander that the Federal artillery was sufficiently disabled to render an assault practicable. One of General Pickett's couriers (Martin Campbell by name) was left with Colonel Alexander to bring his notice to General Pickett whenever he thought the proper time to move had arrived. The artillery duel, as is generally known, raged for about two hours, and at the end of that time there was an evident slacking of the enemy's fire. Colonel Alexander then sent to General Pickett the notice to move, under the impression that the Federal batteries were to some extent silenced. This proved afterward to be a mistake, as a lull in their fire was caused by temporary want of ammunition. When he received the order General Pickett placed himself at the front of his division, actively directing its movements, and in every respect participating in its dangers. In no other positition would it have been possible for him to know what was occuring all along the line, or to discharge the duties which every practical soldier knows would devolve upon a Major General commanding an important movement. When the attack failed he personally superintended the withdrawal of his troops and the formation of the remnant of his division, along a new line near our original position.

That there could possibly have been any doubt as to the facts above mentioned is a matter that will never be comprehended by any man or officer familiar with the facts.

Gettysburg and its Famous Battle.
"Glimpses of America."

The landscape is thereabout undulating, occasionally rising to hills of considerable size. Historically, the place is imperishably famous, for here was fought on the 1st, 2d and 3d of July, 1863, the bloodiest and hottest contested battle of the Civil War. There is Cemetery Hill, the old grave place of the town, where thousands slept before the awakening alarms of cannon and musket enveloped the scene in battle smoke. Here it was that the Union forces under General Meade pitched their quarters because it commanded a view of the adjacent country.

One mile toward the west is Seminary Ridge,
the spot chosen by the Confederates under General
Lee, as their vantage point and headquarters.
Now, sweep the horizon and mark the
places where the battle waxed the fiercest;
where the dead lay thickest and the thunder of
conflict was loudest. Willoughby Run, where
the battle began and where Buford's Cavalry
was hurled upon the steel of Hill, and for two
hours withstood the hell of ball and bayonet
until flesh could endure no more. There is
Round Top, another eminence, where the Union
lines reformed, with the left wing thrown around
the ridge to Cemetery Hill. There is where
Longstreet struck Sickles, with such fearless
resolution, and a whole day was spent in contention
for Great and Little Round Top without
advantage on either side but with frightful
losses to both. Now, on Cemetery Hill the
eyes of the world must rest for here it was on
the third day that such fighting was done as
Greek nor Roman ever knew. After a lull at
midday 200 brazen throats opened with boom
and screaming shells; the air became filled with
smoke and the earth was choked with dead until
there came a lull, out of which broke a column
three miles long. whose gray uniforms
soon proclaimed the advance of General Pickett
leading his army to storm the Union position.

I.—19

No charge ever made was more terrible; no repulse was ever more fatal. Americans, whatever be their sympathies, whatever their prejudices, may feel proud of the .heroism displayed by both armies on that day of carnage around Cemetery Hill. It was a courage that glorifies America. The 54,000 souls that laid down their arms and answered roll call the morning of July 4 on the parade ground of paradise were our countrymen. They were distinguished by uniforms of blue and gray then; they are invested with robes now that are woven without color.

Old and Disabled Veterans.

A RECENT visit to the Confederate Home at Higginsville was repaid by an insight into an institution different in every way from any other. Of course, the attraction of the place is its novelty. The world is full of soldiers' homes —that is, places set apart and maintained by nations. The $100,000 that have been expended here for land and buildings came as voluntary contributions from the men and women of Missouri who admire valor for valor's sake and whose hearts have been touched by the sad plight of the remnant of that brave Spartan

band whose members bared their breasts
in defense of what their fathers had taught
them was right, and who are now suffering for having fought battles and lost. The
inmates have been recruited from every walk of
life. Among the most distinguished recipients
of the kindly hospitality of the home is
Major J. D. Manton. The major has not
been there long, but already he shows the effects
of the quiet life and careful medical attention
afforded by the place. He has a remarkable
history back of him. When a young man,
flushed with the burning pride of the Old South,
he enlisted and equipped at his own expense a
company of cavalry over in the Shenandoah
Valley of Virginia. He was attached to ''Stonewall'' Jackson's command, and was placed on
the staff of that brilliant genius of war as an
aide-de-camp. He was perhaps as close to
Jackson as any man now alive. Taciturn
and imperturbable as a Trappist monk though
Jackson was, he usually talked with his
young aide with a freedom that was sur-
prising to the rest of the staff. '' This
flattered me at first,'' said Major Manton,
''until I found out that the only reason
that Jackson seemed so fond of talking to me
was because I was intimately acquainted with
the country through which we were marching

and he was not. By pumping me in that sly way of his he learned all about the country without letting me know what he was after. Jackson never made a confidant of any man. No one knew what his plans were, if, indeed, he ever knew himself, twelve hours before executing them. Of course the story of his religious devotion is an old one. But I believe I have seen him worshipping his God under circumstances the like of which few men now living witnessed. He never left his tent to lead his men into battle that he did not mumble a prayer, and when in the thickest of the fight, with shells screaming around him, bullets whizzing and whistling, cannon roaring, sabres clashing, men shouting with victory and moaning in the agonies of death, right at the front line of battle could be seen Jackson sitting on his horse, with hands and face upturned to the sky and his thin, pale lips moving in prayer.''

MAKE ONE MORE GUN FOR ME.

[The following poem, written by an Ex-Confederate veteran, was read at the dinner of the Confederate Veteran Camp, of New York, on Monday, the occasion being the anniversary of the birth of Gen. Robert E. Lee.]

Yes, sir; I fought with Stonewall
  And faced the fight with Lee,
But if this here Union goes to war
  Make one more gun for me.

I didn't shrink from Sherman
  As he galloped to the sea,
And if this here Union goes to war
  Make one more gun for me.

I was with them at Manassas,
  The bully boys in gray;
I heard the thunder's roarin'
  Round Stonewall Jackson's way.

And many a time this sword of mine
  Has blazed the route for Lee,
But if this old Union goes to war
  Make one more sword for me.

I'm not so full of fightin',
  Nor half so full of fun
As I was back in sixties
  When I shouldered my old gun.

It may be that my hair is white,
  Such things you know must be,
But if this old Union's in for fight
  Make one more gun for me.

I hain't forgot my raisin',
  Nor how, in sixty-two,

Or thereabouts, with battle shouts,
I charged the boys in blue.

And I say I fought with Stonewall,
And blazed the way with Lee,
But if this old Union's in for war,
Make one more gun for me.

January, 1896.

Just Sound the Tocsin.

I'm not one that hankers muchly for another "cruel war,"
But I don't believe in knucklin' when it's right to stand
up squar;
When a bully wants to bully, whether suitin' you or not,
I'm for dosin' out a potion just to show him what is what!
An' I'm sartin ef the country should be forced at last to
fight
That the legions of the Southland will be found all right.

With the followers of Jackson an' Joe Hooker's men in
line,
Marchin' shoulder unto shoulder, thar'd be bisness, I opine
While the rebel yell of heroes who remain of Lee's com-
mand
Rhymed with wild hurrahs of Spartans left of Grant's un-
daunted band.
Ah! they'd give the world the ager! an' I'd like to see the
fight
Ef it's bound to come upon us—for the South's all right!

Put the soldiers of the sections on the battle-field arrayed,
An' the nation that attacks 'em, needs a coffin ready-made!
They who fought so well at Seven Pines, at Gettysburg,
an' all—

Shakin' fists at danger—smilin' when they heard the battle-
    call.
Don't you know they'd "git thar, Eli"—make a mighty
    winnin' fight,
With the North in real earnest, an' the South all right!

—WILL T. HALE.

"NEVER hand
  Waved sword from stain as free,
  Nor purer sword led braver band,
  Nor braver bled for a brighter land,
  Nor brighter land had a cause so grand,
  Nor a cause a chief like Lee."

" All the bright laurels they fought to make bloom
Fell to the earth when they went to the tomb.
Give them the meed they have won in the past,
Give them the honors their merits forecast;
Give them the chaplets they wore in the strife;
Give them the laurels they lost with their life.
When the great world its last judgment awaits;
When the blue sky shall swing open its gates,
And the long columns march silently through,
Past the Great Captain for final review,
Then for the blood that has flown for the right,
Crowns shall be given untarnished and bright."

Finale

. . . .

My task, though imperfect, incomplete, is ended. Many names are omitted, dear to every Southern heart, worthy to respond to the roll call of fame. It has been, however, more our purpose to offer this tribute to the fallen.

While we accept the "New South" in the spirit of that grand man, Henry Grady, as the flowers bloom 'round peaceful homes to-day and the mocking-birds sing of every clime in these United States, the whippoorwill's plaint in the tangled wood the night "Stonewall" Jackson received his death wound can never be forgotten, and no flowers may ever bloom as sweetly as the *immortelles* planted by loving hands on the graves of the heroes of the " Old South " bedewed by a nation's tears of sorrow.

S. R. R.

𝕴𝖓𝖉𝖊𝖝.

POETRY.